Warwickshire County Council

2 2 OCT 2011			
2 0 SEP 2013			
0 8 APR 2017			
1 2 SEP 2017			

This item is to be returned or renewed before the latest date above. It may be borrowed for a further period if not in demand. **To renew your books:**

- **Phone the 24/7 Renewal Line 01926 499273 or**
- **Visit www.warwickshire.gov.uk/libraries**

Discover • Imagine • Learn • *with libraries*

Also by Joanna Nadin:

Wonderland

paradise

Joanna Nadin

**WALKER
BOOKS**

First published in Great Britain 2011 by Walker Books Ltd
87 Vauxhall Walk, London SE11 5HJ

2 4 6 8 10 9 7 5 3 1

Text © 2011 Joanna Nadin
Front cover photograph © M Thomsen/ Photolibrary.com
Back cover photograph © Moodboard RF/Photolibrary.com

This book has been typeset in Fairfield

Printed and bound in Great Britain by Clays Ltd, St Ives plc

British Library Cataloguing in Publication Data:
a catalogue record for this book is
available from the British Library

ISBN 978-1-4063-2474-7

www.walker.co.uk

For Helen Nadin.

With thanks to Al Greenall
for painting in the gaps.

Secrets

WE ALL have secrets.

Like not liking your best friend that much. But you don't dare tell her because she holds reputations in her hand like eggshell, and if she moves just a finger you're broken, over.

Like keeping your mouth closed when you swig your Bacardi Breezer so she thinks you're as drunk as she is. But when she's not looking you pour half the bottle behind the wall.

The usual stuff.

Even my little brother has secrets. Like he thinks no one knows it was him who drew the solar system on the kitchen ceiling. I knew. But I said nothing. Because those kinds of secrets don't matter. Not really. They're fleeting, like insects, mayflies. Alive for just a day.

But some secrets aren't mayflies. They're monstrous things: skeletons locked in cupboards; notes slipped through the cracks in floorboards and between the pages of books. And, though the ink fades and the paper foxes, the words are still there. Waiting to be found. Or to find us.

If I had known who he was – who *I* was – would it have changed anything? Or would I still have felt that weight on my chest, pushing the air out of my lungs so that, when I saw him, even that first time, I struggled to catch my breath? Would I still have lost hours, nights, thinking about his lips, his slow, lazy smile? And would I still have fallen in love, if I had known?

Maybe. Maybe not. But that's it: I didn't know. Because it was Mum's secret. Het's secret. And, like all skeletons, it came out of the closet. And it found me.

BILLIE

THE KEY arrived three days after Luka left. Mum said it was serendipity. I didn't believe in that kind of stuff, just thought it was a nice word, like *egg*, or *pink*. Back then, anyway. But maybe it *was* serendipity, fate, whatever, because Mum was already kind of losing it. Not big-men-in-white-coats style. Not that time. Just the little things. Like I found her in the kitchen with one of his T-shirts, just standing there, sniffing it. And when I called her Mother as a joke she slammed a glass of Coke down so hard it shattered; shards of transparency scattering across the floor, a slop of soda soaking into a dishcloth.

It wasn't like he was gone for ever – Luka, I mean. He was in Germany with some band for three months – guitarist for a kid half his age and twice his talent, he said. But that wasn't true and he knew it. Luka was good. Which was why he was always getting gigs. Always leaving. He always came back, though. But that wasn't enough for Mum. She said she was tired of it, tired of waiting. She said if he went this time then we might not be here when he knocked on the door come Easter. Luka laughed and said he wouldn't knock; he had a key. He kissed the top of her head and wiped her angry tears with his string-hardened fingers. But she pushed him away and said this time she meant it.

None of us believed her. I mean, he's Finn's dad. She couldn't just disappear, hide. But then the envelope arrived and everything changed.

Mum is out with Finn getting milk and bread and fresh air, or something like it. I say it's too cold, that I don't like fresh air, and I stay in the flat upstairs with the curtains closed and an old Mickey Mouse T-shirt on, and wrap myself up in my duvet and the white-smile world of Saturday-morning telly.

And I'm lying on the sofa watching Tom pot Jerry like he's a snooker ball when I hear the clatter of the letterbox in the shared hallway below, and the post hitting the piles of pizza delivery leaflets, sending them fluttering further across the floor. And I can't remember why, but I get up. Maybe I think it's a postcard from my best friend Cass in the Dominican Republic with her dad and the Stepmonster, getting a tan and another hickey from a boy she'll claim is the love of her life then won't remember when she gets back.

But, when I see it, I know it isn't from Cass. The postmark isn't foreign, but it isn't from round here either. It's a Jiffy envelope, the kind you put fragile stuff in, important stuff; not one of Cass's say-nothing notes, with hearts dotting her *i*s and SWALK on the back. And the writing isn't Biro or pink gel pen; it's black ink, with loops in the *l*s so that "Billie" looks alive. But the name is only half me. Because then the loops spell out "Trevelyan", which is Mum's old surname, before she changed it – changed us – to "Paradise", a word Mum picked up from a sign above a shop door on Portobello. Kept it the way you keep a glass marble. Because she liked the way it felt in her mouth. Because she thought a name could make it happen, make it real.

I feel this surge of fear inside me. No, not fear exactly, thrill. The kind you get on a rollercoaster. Or when someone double-dares you to down a shot. Bad and good all wrapped up in one sickening whirl. And suddenly I'm small and scared, standing in my T-shirt and socks on the bare concrete, and I have to look around to check if anyone has seen me, if Mrs Hooton from Flat B is coming out in her slippers and threadbare dressing-gown to catch me with this— What? This thing in my hand. But I'm alone, and I shiver, the January air an icy hiss through the gaps around the door, stippling my thighs and arms with goosepimples. And I run back up the stairs and slam the door and pull the duvet around me again, still holding the envelope, hot in my hand like Frodo's ring.

I think even then I knew it. That it wasn't just a package. It was a talisman, a magic amulet to change my world.

I duck my head under the cover and roll onto my side, the light from the telly shining through the faded polyester flowers, so that I can open the envelope and wait for the power to seep out and transform my life.

And it almost does.

It's a key. Not like ours. Not a shiny Chubb that locks out Mrs Hooton and the rest of the world. Locks us in. But the old kind. Heavy, blackened iron. The kind you get in fairy tales that opens up a haunted mansion in the woods, or a box of cursed treasure, or the Ark of the Covenant. And when I read the letter, with it pressing its cold metallic print into my palm, it feels electric. Because it *is* a fairy tale. Only it's real. And it's about me.

The story is simple, short. Typed in sharp Times New Roman on a single page. A woman has died. Eleanor Trevelyan. My grandmother. She has died and left me a house. Cliff House. In Seaton. In Cornwall.

I have inherited a house. The one Mum grew up in, and left sixteen years ago, when I was already inside her. Because I was already inside her.

Seaton. Sea Town. I sound the words out silently in my head. Picturing this strange place. This palace. And I feel that feeling again, that thrill. Because I know I should be pale and grieving for this lost dead woman. But the thing is: I have never met her. I kind of knew she existed. I mean, obviously my mum had to have a mother, and a father, though he's long gone. She had a brother, too: Will. But he died. And I came. And Mum left and now she won't talk about it.

So instead of crying, I laugh. Because it's funny. It's fairytale funny. Because I live in this two-and-a-bit-bedroom flat in Peckham with no carpet and a boiler that only works when it feels like it, and all along I have a house, a castle by the sea. I'm not the Little Match Girl, I'm Cinderella.

But then I hear the front door bang against the wall and Finn's voice one long stream of Gogo's and Jedis and "Did you see that?"'s, and I remember who I am. I'm not Cinderella. Or Sleeping Beauty. I'm Billie. And Mum's mother has died and she doesn't even know, and I'm scared to tell her because every time I've mentioned her before, just casual, she has ignored me or yelled at me, or, worse, taken it out silently on herself. So I stuff the key and the letter back in the envelope and push them down the back of the sofa cushion. And they stay there for three whole days.

I thought about not telling Mum at all. I mean, I'm sixteen. I could just go and live there on my own. Live this incredible enchanted life in my castle by the sea. That's what Cass said anyway. Or, better, I could sell it and buy somewhere up West. So we could go to Chinawhite's instead of Chicago's. But as she sat on the end of my bed, in her St Tropez tan, I knew every nod, every "yeah" was a lie.

I knew I'd tell in the end. Had to. Because my mum's not like Cass's, who doesn't know Cass lost her virginity when she was thirteen. That it was to Leon Drakes and she wasn't in love or anything like it. That she got pregnant and paid for an abortion with the money her dad sends her every month. The money she still spends on dope and drink and the slots at Magic City.

And even the stuff Cass's mum does know she doesn't really register. Because if she did, she wouldn't let Cass do half of what she does.

But my mum's different. My mum you tell stuff to. And this was big stuff. Family stuff. And the longer I left it, the worse it got. Because the key was like the tell-tale heart in that story we did for GCSE. This guy buries the heart of a murdered man under the floorboards, only he's sure he can still hear it beating, this *thump thump thump*, and it slowly drives him mad.

And maybe it's just my own heart, but I swear I can hear that key beating its presence, pulsing it out like heat. Like a heart. I look at Finn and Mum to see if they can hear it too. And even though Finn just carries on laughing at the cartoons and Mum flicks another page in a magazine, I know it is only a matter of time.

By Tuesday I can't stand it any longer. I'll be back at school tomorrow and I don't want to leave Mum alone in the house with it. Don't know what she'll do if she finds it. As it is, I hide the big knife in the kitchen. Just in case.

I don't say anything, just hand the envelope to her at breakfast, with this look on my face like I'm giving her my school report and there's not even a C on it, let alone a B. I feel Finn yank my sleeve, hear him demand to know what it is, but I shrug him off because I'm watching Mum, hidden under her shroud of dirty blonde, her knees inside the black mohair of one of Luka's sweaters, bare feet poking out. And I wait.

When she got a letter telling her that her father had died, she said nothing. Just shrugged and dropped it in the bin and went back to buttering toast. But this is different, I think. This is her mother. She was inside her once. Part of her. She has to lose it.

But she doesn't, just stretches her legs to the floor and turns her head to me. And as she pushes her hair behind one ear, I see she is smiling.

"I should have told you before," I say. "I mean, I meant to. It's just— I didn't know what you would—"

"It's fine," she interrupts. "Really."

"We don't have to live there. Cass says I could sell it – we could sell it, I mean. Pay the back rent here. Or buy it even. Or one of those big houses on the Grove near Cass and—"

"No," she says. "It's a sign. It's serendipity. We'll go. We'll move."

My stomach is alive again. Butterflies battering against the sides trying to get out.

"What's serendipity?" asks Finn. "And where are we going?"

"Fate," she replies. "Good fate. And it's taking us to the seaside."

"Like Margate? Will there be donkeys? Can we stay for dinner?"

"Yes." She nods. "Yes, there's donkeys. And yes, we can stay. Not just for dinner though. For the night. For a thousand and one nights." And her smile widens, as if she's just realized what she's said.

Finn yelps with delight and flings himself onto Mum. I watch as she basks in his adoration. Then, infected by his eight-year-oldness, she wraps him round her and stands, dancing him across the painted floor, Finn screaming as she whirls to the tinny sound of the radio. But I don't dance. Instead the butterflies surge upwards and I have to fight to push them down.

"And Dad will come?" Finn says, breathless. "And we can swim in the sea like sharks?"

"Yes," Mum says, her eyes closed, still dancing. But I know she doesn't mean it. This is her escape. Her get-out-of-jail-free card. "We don't need anyone. We have us." That's what she always said, even before Finn came. "Us is what matters. We are all the family we need."

And part of me believes her. That it's just us. And that home will be wherever we want it to be. But then I think about Cass. Who I've known since for ever. Who bought me my first Beanie Baby. My first tampons. My first drink. About Luka. Who's not my dad, but is the closest I've ever got. And as good as I'd ever want.

"It's my key," I say in desperation.

Mum stops and lowers Finn down, one arm round him, the other reaching out to stroke my face.

"I know," she says. "And it's your decision."

"Please, Billie," begs Finn. "Please."

I look at him, his eyes wide with worry, scared I'll shatter his sand-covered peppermint-rock-flavoured dream.

"I'll think about it," I say. "I need to think about it."

But as Mum pulls us tight to her and carries us round, the ceiling a kaleidoscope of broken light bulb and damp and purple-felt-tip planets, I know I'm losing the fight.

Het

SHE TELLS them not because she wants to, but because she has to. Because Tom has begged her, and because she knows there is no other way.

Maybe she will feel a weight lifted, she thinks. Maybe relief will wash over her. Like the problem pages say it will. But Het can see them in her mind's eye, the women at the magazines, in their glossy world, rose-tinted glasses with their glasses half full, always half full.

And Het's glass is empty.

Her mother touches three polished fingers to her lips, trying to catch the "Oh, Hetty" that escapes from them. But Het hears it, hears the fear.

Her father says nothing. Lets nothing out. Just stands there for a second, his jaw set with tension, straining to contain his rage, his disappointment and disgust. Then he turns and walks out of the room, slamming the door behind him.

Eleanor flinches at the sound, at the gust of air that scatters a sheaf of papers across a side table and onto the carpet. Het waits for her to say something. To do something. To hold her, to say it's going to be all right.

But instead she stands quickly, scoops up the stray papers and places them neatly in a pile back on the table. Then walks smartly out of the room.

It's not going to be all right.

Het is lying on her bed when she hears the tread of the stairs. Two sets of feet, one in black brogues, size ten, one smaller, in heels. She has learned their rhythms, their meanings over the years. The prickling irritation of one; the threat of the other.

Het looks at the shoes in the frame of the doorway. Like policemen, she thinks. Bringing bad news.

"I have made an appointment for you," he tells her.

"It will be quick," Eleanor adds. "Over with."

Het looks up from the floor. "I'm keeping it," she says simply.

"But—" her mother starts.

"The university won't allow it," he interrupts. Then slower, calmer: "I won't allow it."

Het turns over to face the window. "It's not up to you."
She watches as this sinks in. Then adds the punchline: "Any-
way, I'm not going back."

"But all your hard work..." Eleanor gasps. "It's what you
always wanted."

"No," Het says calmly. "It's what you always wanted."

For seven seconds there is silence. Het counts them. One
elephant, two elephant... Then the door closes and the feet
tread their familiar step along the corridor, but quicker now;
then another door slams, and Het can hear raised voices,
accusations, blame, the heavy slap of a hand against a rouged
cheek. She pulls a pillow over her head and fills her glass
another way. Fills it with him.

Two weeks, he said. Enough time for him to earn some money
from the fair. For Martha to find them somewhere to stay.

Two weeks and she will be gone. She will leave all this
weight, this dull aching impossible life behind. And she will
be his. For ever.

BILLIE

I'M SITTING in my bedroom, curtains open, London night seeping in through the gaps in the broken sash window. The sound of traffic, the smell of fried food, the shrieks of hamburger-happy girls bathed in the golden glow of McDonald's. Sheer teeming life that dances down the dirty pavements twenty-four hours a day. My life. A life I'm not sure I want to leave for a dead-end seaside town.

It's different for Finn. He's a kid. All he can see is candyfloss and the big dipper and donkeys on the sand. But what would I do there? Who would I be?

Cass says she'd kill to get out of London, live by the sea, with her year-round tan and surfers checking her out, waiting on her every move. But the beaches she's lain on are in Corfu not Cornwall. And she'd never leave London anyway. Not if it came down to it. She says she feels dizzy if she has to go to Zone 3. And when our year went to Windsor Castle for the day, she told Mr Hegarty she got travel-sick and stayed behind in the library all day. She *is* London. She'd fade like a hothouse flower if you took her out of the noise and the dirt. And I wonder if I'd be like that. If I'd shrink even further into myself. If I'd wither. Stop breathing. And I add it to my list of excuses.

"I like London," I say to Mum. "It's alive. There's museums and art galleries and stuff." Every word practised, knowing that this has been her argument in the past. Her reason for coming, for staying.

But not now, not any more. Mum says London is a bad place to raise a kid. She means Finn. "But what about me?" I say. "You raised me here. What's so wrong with how I turned out?" But then I think of the time she and Luka came home early one night and Cass was in their bedroom with Ash Johnson. You'd have thought it was me in there, the way she went off. And I said I'd begged Cass not to. But it's hard to say no to her. And I remember what Mum said: that Cass was a bad influence, out of control. And what she didn't say: that maybe I would go the same way. And I think, Mum one, Billie nil.

I say, "What about school? I can't just leave after one term of A levels."

But Mum says there's schools there. And they won't have to use dog-food tins instead of Pyrex jars in science, won't have a crèche for all the Year Elevens who've had kids.

I say, "If they're that good then they'll be full."

But Mum says she can home-school until a place comes up.

And I'm three points down.

The next morning I try again.

"You hate the sea," I say.

And it's true. That time in Margate she sat up high on the sand, her back to the stone wall of the promenade, like she was fastened. A shell. Wouldn't even let the water spread over her toes. Luka had to take me and Finn into the shallows.

"I did," she says. "But it's different now. It's all different, don't you see? Don't you understand?"

And I nod. Because I want her to think we're still all right. But I don't. Understand, I mean. Why she wants it so bad. Why she wants to go back to the place she's run from for sixteen years. To the people. She's the one who's always saying stuff like "It's not where you come from, Billie, it's where you're going that matters" and "You can choose who you want to be. Who do you want to be, Billie?"

But I don't know. Who I am. Or who I want to be.

I slump on my elbows and look at myself in the mirror. See me surrounded in the flyblown glass, draped with necklaces; gig passes and notes from Cass Blu-Tacked to the chipped gold frame. Who am I? I think. Then I cringe at myself, at how lame it sounds. Like one of those self-help books that Mum's friend Martha reads, or some *High School Musical* shlock. Only it's not a book or a film. It's real.

And, as I stare at my reflection – at my hair, lank and dark, the opposite of Mum's thick, wild blonde; at my pale skimmed-milk skin – I wonder if she's wrong. If it's a lie that the past doesn't matter. Because we're made up of our past. Of our parents. I think of Finn. And I can see which bits are Mum – the same hair, the same smile; and which are Luka's – his brown eyes, his wide hands – guitarist hands, Luka says. But when I look at me, there's this stranger.

Then something clicks inside me. This little switch. Or a seed. Like the pink and black of a runner bean, it splits and something grows. A need. And I pull open a drawer and scrabble under the postcards and the Tube tickets and the pink Post-its to find what I'm looking for. A blank piece of paper. And a pencil. And I start to draw. But not all of me. I take away the bits that are Mum, the cat eyes, the too-big lips that she hates, and Luka loves.

I only draw what I don't know. My nose, the high forehead, the hair. But when I look at the sketch, at what's left, it's like one of those photofits on *Crimewatch*. Or that kids' game where you slot different face sections in. Nothing fits. I can't see him.

I know nothing about Tom. My dad. Never have. Just that Mum loved him, and he left. I don't know how tall he is, what colour his hair is. I'm guessing pretty tall, because I've already got six centimetres on Mum. And dark. But I don't know for sure. There are no photos. No letters. And Mum doesn't talk about him any more than she talks about Will or her parents. I have no idea who he was. Maybe an artist. Because this must come from somewhere. Like Finn's guitar hands. These things don't just happen, and Mum can't draw. Her birds are like aliens. Blobs with slits for eyes and wings in the wrong places. But I know I'm good. Good enough, anyway.

And for the first time in a long time I want to know. Because I figure unless I know who he is, I don't know who I am. Or who I want to be. And that's when I decide we can go. Because I want to find him. To find me.

HET

HET SITS at her mother's dressing-table. She is ten. Too young to be wearing the lipstick that coats her mouth and cheeks; thick red grease, like a clown child. Too young for the cloud of Chanel that surrounds her. Too young, too, for the tears that are trickling down her cheeks, taking a layer of soot-black mascara with them, running rivulets to her chin before dripping noiselessly onto the white smocking of her dress.

You can't cry in a mirror, she remembers. Can't cry if you look at yourself. And so she stares hard at her reflection, willing the tears, this feeling, to stop. But Will's fact is a lie after all. Or she is the exception. A freak. An aberration.

She blinks away the inky salt of her tears and looks harder. She has her mother's eyes, her mouth. Just like Will.

So why is she so different? She repeats her father's words silently to herself: "Why can't you be more like your brother?" But the Het in the mirror doesn't know either, just shrugs and lets another Elizabeth Arden tear stain her collar.

Why can't she be like him? Why can't she feel like he does? Why can't she dig for lugworms with Jonty, screaming with laughter as they disappear further into the waterlogged sand, too quick for the steel of the spade? Why can't she wake happy that the sun is drenching her bedspread, filling everyone it touches with drunken joy, pulling them to the beach, to the fairground, into cafés and arcades? Everyone except her. Why, instead, does she feel this greyness that not even lipstick can hide? This weight that keeps her inside the cold, quiet granite of the house and pins her to her bed for hours, staring wordlessly at a crack in the plaster?

Then she hears the creak as her mother's heels dig into the wide staircase, feels the minute change in air pressure. And Het stops sniffing and silently slips to the floor, crawling under the lace-edged valance of her parents' bed, where she will stay for two hours, until her father's anger-soaked baritone chases her out for supper.

BILLIE

FOR A MINUTE I think I'm going to bottle it. When we're sitting at Paddington: I think, I could do it. I could get off the train right now. Go to Cass's. Or back to the flat.

Mr Garroway doesn't even know we've gone yet. Mum doesn't want to ring. Knows he'll come round and demand the back rent there and then. Rent we don't have. Not yet. She says he'll find out soon enough when he turns up and all that's left is an empty flat and a boiler that's on the blink.

Before we left, I looked around: at the pencil notches on the kitchen wall marking off the months and years of Finn's growth in centimetre increments. Day-Glo magnets clinging to the fridge – the *f, i* and *n*s long missing – spelling out nonsense words now, gobbledegook. A picture of a horse by a seven-year-old me that I glued to the door because we'd run out of Blu-Tack. Pieces of us.

"But not us," Mum says. "None of it. Just ephemera."

I looked it up. It's an insect, a mayfly that only lives for a day or something. But I know what she means. I know why she made us pack the rest up and take bagful after bagful to the charity shop. Not just because of the train. But because all that matters is us: me, her and Finn. Stuff comes and goes. We are our own world and possessions.

"What about my chair?" Finn begs.

Mum looks at the tiny wooden thing, made by his grandpa, his "Nonno" – Luka's dad. Too small for Finn to squeeze into now so a plush giraffe and Buzz Lightyear lie tangled together on the worn pine, an improbable pair. "There'll be furniture there," she says. "Or we can get new stuff."

What with? I think. Mum hasn't got a job. Hasn't had one for a year now. And before that they only lasted a few months before she'd start turning up late, or not at all. Or argue and get fired. But I don't say anything. Because I know what she's doing. She's starting again. She wants new things. New people. And so I fit my world into two suitcases. My jeans, the denim soft and faded with two years of washing, but Cass's name in a heart stubbornly in-grained in black Bic on the knee; my cowboy boots that I begged for for months because Cass had a pair; my paints and sketch-pad, every page filled with graphite lines: Finn eating a Cornetto, the ice cream trickling down his chin; Luka sitting at the table, playing guitar. Moments gone. Dead. I push the pad down to the bottom of the blue vinyl. My secret.

Cass comes over to say goodbye. She's crying, crocodile tears welling in the corners of her eyes then slipping over her waterproof mascara, saying how I have to get a mobile because it's my human right and Mum is abusing me or lying even that they'll radiate my brain but if I don't then she'll email or write even, like in a film, with proper paper and everything. Then she checks her make-up in the mirror, the gold frame exposed, naked, the notes binned, necklaces hanging in the Salvation Army. Says she has to go because she's meeting Stella down at Chicago's. Then she gets up and hugs me, and fans her eyes, as if she's willing the tears to stay in. But I know she won't cry again, because there's only so much that her Maybelline can take, and because Ash is going to be at Chicago's, too. I know this because she's wearing a crop top, her tan tummy a flash of brown goosebumps between the red check and denim blue.

And I don't cry either. Not then. Not when we close the door for the last time and leave the note on Mrs Hooton's mat; not on the 36 when we pass Oliver Goldsmith Primary where Cass and I first met; not when we're on Vauxhall Bridge and I look down the river at the Eye and the Houses of Parliament and the picture-postcard London.

But now, sat on the InterCity on Platform 5, my eyes fill with tears, as my head fills with insects, the mayflies we're leaving behind. I think of Luka coming back to the flat to find someone else in our place and his stuff in a box in the hallway. Of Finn's "Nonno" and "Nonna", in a flat just a mile from here, Polaroids of Finn and me grinning out from the silver frames that crowd their windowsills like an army of memories. And I'm scared that we will die and disappear; that they won't care; that we are ephemera too. And I'm scared we're not; that we are more than fragile wings and faded photographs; that part of them will be missing for ever.

I hear the shrill note of the guard's whistle, the last-minute clatter of bags and feet on the platform before the doors are slammed, and I am suddenly aware I am trapped in this tin carriage, being taken away from my life to a new one I'm not even sure I want. The insects are in my stomach now, and I stand suddenly, nauseous, panicking.

"Billie?" Mum questions.

"I need the loo," I say. I lurch down the aisle, pushing past tutting men in suits, clutching at the backs of seats to steady myself and push me closer to the exit. My cases are at the bottom of the luggage rack. Too heavy to pull out now. Not enough time. They're just stuff, I say to myself.

But when I get there, when I'm standing at the open window, my lungs heaving, my knuckles white, gripped around the cold metal of the handle, I think of him. Of the part of me that's missing. Not even a Luka, coming and going in and out of my life. Never there at all. My hand relaxes on the handle, blood rushing back to the tips of my fingers, and I look up to meet the eyes of the guard, his whistle touching his lips, waiting to see which way I'm going to go. I drop my hand and pull it inside the window. And the guard closes his mouth around the whistle and blows.

I'm back in my seat as the train pulls out of the station. Past the stucco terraces, past the horses under the Westway. Past the tower block with the Polaroid army on the windowsill. Finn sees it too. Asks if Nonno and Nonna can come and stay. "Yeah, course," says Mum. But she's not really listening. She's not really here. She's somewhere else, in another carriage, another time.

Because she did it before. Caught a train along this line, but on the other side of the tracks. Left home and came to London. She erased her world, her past. Now she's doing it again. Rubbing out the flat and the debt and the never-quite-enough of Luka.

But then I remember something Luka said about the past. That it never really goes away, that it catches up with you, grasping at your ankles and pulling you back. Wherever you hide, it will find you in the end. And I wonder if it's found Mum. If this is a new start. Or if she's going back to the start.

Het

HET WAKES *and pulls up the thick cotton blind on the sleeper car. The night-shrouded fields and grey granite walls she left behind have given way to early sunlight and the 1930s red-brick world of West London. She heaves herself upright on the narrow bunk and lets her legs drop to the floor. Leaden with sleep, they bang against the leather of her bag.*

She touches her belly, swelling now, aware that she hasn't eaten for hours, since last night. Her last supper. Cold, boiled ham and beans from the garden. Eaten in silence, save for the ticking of the grandfather clock in the hall, marking out the seconds and minutes until she could leave this family of strangers behind.

Her stomach gurgles and she looks up, embarrassed. But

the bunk above her is empty. She is alone.

She roots around in the front pocket of her bag until her fingers find what she is looking for. She pulls out a stick of peppermint rock and unwraps the cellophane. A slip of paper flutters to the floor, a black-and-white beach scene and the words A GIFT FROM SEATON. Het sees it but doesn't pick it up. In an hour it will be swept away, ephemera. Like the pink letters stretching through the rock, Seaton will disappear, will be sucked into sweet sugary nothing. What's real, what matters, is what's in front of her. Martha's flat, and London, and this new life inside her. Her new life.

BILLIE

I **WAKE** up with the sound of rain hammering against the reinforced glass, Mum's breath warm in my ear, whispering that we're here. I open my eyes to the fluorescent glare of the carriage. Outside it's pitch black, late now. I strain to see the landscape, but all I can make out is my own bleary-eyed reflection. The train is slowing, the wet iron of the rails squealing a protest as its brakes lock on. I stare at the window and slowly my sleep-soaked face, Finn's excitement, Mum's expectation all melt away under the orange sodium glow of the platform lights, and we see where we are, where we're going. Black letters on white, spelling out our new world: SEATON.

"Are we here? Are we?" Finn demands, though he can read as well as me.

Mum smiles. "We're here. Come on. Get the bags."

"It's raining," I say, disappointment taking the edge off the fear I feel.

For a second I think I see a glimpse of it in Mum too. But, if it's there, she forces practicality to push it down.

"We'll get a cab."

"Like on holiday," says Finn.

Mum laughs. "Just like on holiday."

But, even with our suitcases, and the tang of sea in the air, I don't feel like I'm on holiday. This isn't the newness of Margate, or Majorca. This is something else; older, deeper. And if I feel it, who have never been here before, except as a tiny seed inside her, then Mum must feel it too.

I lean into her in the back of the cab, feel her arm snake round me, the other already holding Finn, pulling him down into his seat as he strains to find the sand and the sea and the donkeys.

"What do you think?" she asks.

I look out at night-shuttered shops and arcades, neon signs with bulbs missing so that Tenpenny Falls is cut price to a penny; El Dorado an illegible scrawl, and I think of Magic City. Cass and Ash playing the slots and drinking cheap lager from brown paper bags.

"Like Peckham," I say. "But wetter."

The rain drums against the roof of the taxi, sweeping over the windscreen in a sudden, blinding arc as we turn out of the town centre and begin to climb a steep hill.

"It's not always this bad," the cabbie says. The first words he's spoken, save for the "Where to?" at the station and the grunt as he heaved six suitcases into the boot of his rusting Ford Mondeo.

"Oh I know," says Mum. "I grew up here."

The cabbie snorts. Meaning what? That she doesn't talk or look like she grew up here. That we're outsiders. That we'll never fit in. Thoughts that will prick me, prod at me again and again in the weeks and months ahead. But right now I bat the accusing fingers away. Because the cab has stopped. We're here.

Cliff House towers over us, important. Solid granite walls, stained glass in the door, dark now, but in my head I see it backlit with the warmth of a chandelier. It isn't a palace. Not really. There are no turrets, no arrow slots for windows. But, even in the rain and half-light, it's a fairy tale. So far from the flat in Peckham that I have to choke back a laugh. Because how can I have grown up there, and Mum here? How can she have given up all this for so little? But even as I ask I know the answer. Because I was what mattered. Not five bedrooms, and two floors, and a garden the size of a park. Because they would have been empty without me there. And they didn't want me there. Until now.

Mum shakes me from my imagined palace. "Have you got the key?" she asks frantically, the contents of her purse tinkling onto the black and white tiles of the path as she upends it in the search.

For a second I panic. That I have forgotten it. That it is sitting laughing to itself on the scratched kitchen table in Peckham. But then I remember slipping it into the pocket of my black dress, its weight pulling the fabric, threatening to pull the stitches away from the seam. I push my hand inside, and it is there, the metal pressing against my hip bone.

"Here," I say, and I hold it out to her.

"No, you do it," Mum replies, still picking up the cab change from the floor, precious coins that she knows we need, though she'll spend them without thought.

"Let me," begs Finn. "I'll do it."

"No," says Mum. "It's Billie's, remember."

"'S'OK," I shrug. And it is. Because I don't want to do it. In case it doesn't fit. Or it is the Ark of the Covenant, or Pandora's Box, letting out something wonderful and terrible all at once.

But none of this happens. The key fits, and instead of shrieking, I hear the satisfying clunk as the frame releases its grip on the door and it swings heavily, silently open.

Finn looks up for a light switch and finds one, a brown Bakelite circle, a relic from another age. He pulls it down with a sharp click.

"Wow," he says. And for once I am caught up in his fever. Because, even though the floor is strewn with post, this isn't the bare concrete of the flat hallway. This floor is criss-crossed in wooden parquet, like one of those Magic Eye paintings, concealing a secret pattern. And beyond that, carpet takes over, not the rough hessian mats that mark your knees and wear holes in your socks, but actual soft, sage-green carpet.

"Don't just stand there all night," says Mum. "Come on."

I turn to look at her. Trying to read her. But all I can make out is impatience and cold.

"I'm hungry," says Finn, and he instinctively stoops to scoop up the post. "Can we have pizza?"

"It's too late," laughs Mum. "And I don't even think they deliver food here. It's not like London. People cook."

Finn shrugs and heads down the hall. To check the fridge, I assume. I turn back to Mum, still framed in the doorway, her hair a halo, the wind and rain a *Wuthering Heights* backdrop to the wild Cathy standing before me. I hesitate. But I need to know.

"Are you OK?" I ask.

Mum tips her head to one side. As if she might tell me a secret. But instead, she rolls her eyes. "I'm knackered," she says. "And this wind is hideous." She slams the door behind her and follows Finn.

The fridge is empty but Mum starts rooting in cupboards. "Pasta?" she says, holding up a half-full packet of penne.

"With what?" asks Finn.

She looks again and finds a bottle of ketchup and a tin of tuna. Finn pulls a face. But she kisses it away. "It'll be lovely," she says. "We ate it all the time when I was a student." And she opens the packet and pours it, clattering, into an expensive-looking saucepan from an overhead rack.

"Can I look round?" asks Finn.

Mum nods, dropping the packet without thought into the bin under the sink. Finn disappears into the house, his feet a soft thud on the carpet fading up the stairs.

Mum looks at me. "Go on," she says. "You can go too, if you want."

So I do.

Finn finds it first. I hear him call "Bagsy" and I know he's claiming the best bedroom. The biggest one. Or the one with the sea view. Or the secret passage.

But the secret's bigger than that.

The walls are covered with certificates. Awards for swimming, for rugby, for rowing. Silver trophies glint and wink on polished shelves. And by the bed a stack of *Beano*s sits waiting to be read.

But not by Finn. By Will.

The room looks like it hasn't changed since the day he died. The bed made. The curtains drawn. His shoes lined up neatly in a row against the wall. A shrine to a boy who went before I was even born. And I realize she lived like this for sixteen years. Eleanor. My grandmother. One child gone away. And one dead. Nothing more than ghosts.

But ghosts haunt you. And I think of Mum downstairs. And I run.

*   *   *

"Mum," I blurt.

"What?" Mum looks up. But her face is serene. She's seen nothing.

"I... It doesn't matter."

Mum shrugs and lights the gas stove. And I watch her moving around this kitchen, like she's never been away. Like it's hers. Yet it's so clearly not. The surfaces are uncluttered, the painted oak cupboards free of Blu-Tacked photos, the melamine clean, no knife tracking its surface because someone can't be bothered to find a chopping board. I wonder about the last time she was in here. And I wonder where she's put the memories. If she's boxed them away. Or left them behind like so much unwanted furniture.

Finn comes back full of things he's found, the elephant's tusk and the stuffed bird, and *can he have the bedroom at the back?* Mum smiles, says he can have anything he wants. And as we sit down to eat she calls it our banquet, a feast fit for a king. And I smile and think, This is OK; this is good. She's good.

It's gone eleven when we're done, plates piled unwashed on the drainer, ketchup trailing a syrupy drip down the glass bottle onto the table, water puddle on the floor where I turned the tap on too far. Already we're making our mark.

"So, bed," announces Mum.

"No," protests Finn. "I want to see the garden."

Mum laughs. "It's too dark, and you're too tired."

"I'm not," he insists, predictably. But his eyelids are half closed, his skin pale, ghostlike. More like me now, I think.

"Go on," she says. "You can leave your teeth tonight. Do them harder in the morning."

"Yes!" Finn has scored a cup-winning goal and races off, up the stairs to his new bedroom.

"Where shall I sleep?" I ask.

Mum is scraping leftovers onto her plate, doesn't even look up. "Up the stairs, to the left. Last one along the corridor. My old room," she adds.

I pause, confused. "Don't you want it?"

She shakes her head, lets her eyes meet mine. "I'll sleep in the spare room. It's bigger."

"Oh, thanks." I feign hurt. "Are you coming?"

"I'll be up in a bit," she says. "You go. Really."

She's going to have a smoke. Keeps the packet behind the radio at home, does it late at night out of the kitchen window when she thinks we're asleep. But I can smell it on her, tangled in her hair in the morning. Another secret.

"Night, then," I say, and I lean down to kiss her.

Mum tilts her cheek to my lips, and I feel her breath against my own as she whispers, "Night, Billie."

And I'm not sure what more to say, so I leave her, sitting at the table she sat at sixteen years ago, her head full of something, or nothing, and I climb the wide galleried staircase. I wonder what I will find at the top: a four-poster with a canopy draping around, a tiny replica pram full of porcelain dolls, a princess's chamber; or a room full of teen-age Mum, posters for bands I've seen on *Top of the Pops 2*, a wardrobe packed with ra-ra skirts and batwing tops.

But it's neither. It's just yellow wallpaper, clean and bare, not even a drawing-pin hole marking its faint, flowered pattern, and a single wooden bed. The wardrobe and shelves are empty, the windowsill home to nothing more than a scattering of dust.

At first I think I've got it wrong. That I took a wrong turn on the landing and this is the spare room. But I check again, and this is it: left at the top of the stairs, last room along. I don't get it. I saw Will's room. Like any day he would walk back in the door and it would be ready for him, nothing moved, nothing thrown away. Yet Mum's has been scoured clean. As if she's the one who died. The one they needed to forget.

But I'm too tired to think for long. Too tired to dig in my bag for a clean T-shirt. Instead, I peel off my jumper and tights and crawl under the crackling white sheets and wool blankets, ready to curl into sleep. But as I draw my legs up, my knee brushes against something. I gasp, and freeze, scared I've found a dead cat. Or a live demon.

But there's no smell, no sound, no heat. Whatever it is, it's nothing, I think. It is benign. So, slowly, carefully, I reach down and feel the nap of velvet against my fingers. When I pull it out I see it's not a demon. But it's not nothing either. It's a toy. A rabbit. Mum's rabbit. And I fall asleep with it clutched to my chest.

ELEANOR

ELEANOR STANDS in the doorway, her shoulders hanging, a roll of bin-bags in her right hand; the thumb of her left playing with her wedding ring, a thin, pale band of gold, turning it this way and that. This cannot be right, she thinks. A lifetime, nineteen years of Het. All of it to be wrapped in black plastic. Discarded like a cracked teapot.

Eleanor stiffens. He is behind her now. She can smell the alcohol rub from the day's surgery, hear the laboured breathing, a soft rasp she once feared, and now hopes, is something more than just middle age.

"All of it," he says.

She hesitates, trying to find an excuse he will accept, knowing that sentiment will be swatted like a lazy bluebottle.

"But it's such a waste," she protests, finally. "Can't we at least save it for charity?"

"She's gone," he says. "Dead. You bury the dead."

The following day he drives eight black bin-bags to the refuse site and lays her to rest in a yellow council skip. Her nineteen years worth no more than someone's shattered mirror and four paint-chipped chairs.

In Het's doorway, Eleanor twists her wedding ring. In her right hand she is clutching something else. A soft, velveteen thing, with long ears and a cotton-wool scut. A thing forgotten, or hidden. She hears wheels crunching on gravel, his Jaguar, its soft engine no longer purring a welcome but a warning. Quickly, quietly, Eleanor holds the toy to her face and breathes Het in for the last time, a fusty, child smell. A smell of years of love. Of life. Then she pushes it down beneath the crisp sheets of the single bed, made up now for guests who will never visit. If he finds it, what will she say? That it was a mistake. That she must have missed it in her hurry. That Rose, the housekeeper, must have done it; one of her superstitions.

But he doesn't find it. It is another secret, another skeleton. Slipped through a crack for someone to dig up and piece together later.

BILLIE

I WAKE to the sound of rain against glass. Groaning inwardly I pull back thick chintz curtains – the old kind, not the shabby-chic ones I've seen in Luka's Sunday supplements – and look down on a town bathed in grey, impossible to see where the granite terraces end and the mist begins. I know the sea is out there somewhere, beyond all this. Can hear its white noise against the harder drum of raindrops and thrum of traffic. But for now I may as well be back in Peckham for all the hot sand, sun-bleached dreams I can touch.

I wonder if it ever stops here, the rain. The house seems steeped in damp: the windowsill ripe with a dark spattering of mould; that earthy smell in the cupboards. It's cold, too, so that my breath fogs up in a cloud around my face and, when I pee, steam rises from the toilet bowl. I touch the wide, white-painted bathroom radiator. Nothing. The boiler is broken. Or the heating hasn't clicked on yet. I try to remember last night. Was it like this when we got here? Or were we too distracted with newness to notice? I tread back along the sea-green soft corridor to my room to pull on yesterday's tights and jumper. Then add a long, moth-eaten cardigan. One of Mum's cast-offs, Luka's before that. Cass used to laugh at it. Said it looked like a dead man's clothes, like something out of the Sally Army shop. Mum agreed. Said I should bin it; it was more hole than cardigan. But I defended it. Claimed it was vintage. And I guess it is, in a way. But that's not why I love it. I pull it tight around me, wrapping myself in its thick, wool softness, and the smell of him and her. That's what I'm holding on to. Not the thing. But what it means. What inhabits it.

When I get downstairs Mum and Finn are up and eating breakfast. I watch as Finn bites into a doughnut, sugar coating his lips, grease and jam oozing down his fingers. The sentinel ketchup bottle has been joined by cartons of milk; pots of honey and lemon curd; a half-empty teacup; a pat of butter, its whiteness already plundered by a gouging knife and traces of something that looks like Marmite.

We're the Railway Children, I think. Finding only empty cupboards, then waking the next day to apple pie that has been missed in the dark of their arrival.

"Where was it?" I ask.

Finn pulls a face. Answers, still chewing, "Duh. Like, in the shop."

I look at Mum. She is wearing a dress, cut low, flakes of croissant decorating her chest.

"We went out exploring," she says. "Found Aladdin's Cave."

"It's actually called that," Finn adds. "But the man doesn't look like Aladdin, he looks like Fat Al from the corner shop."

"They've got everything," Mum says. "Croissants. Olives. Can you believe it? I never saw an olive until I moved to London but now they've got jars of them."

I click.

"You should have gone to the supermarket," I say. "I bet it cost a ton."

"Oh lighten up, Billie." Mum holds out a packet of pains au chocolat. "Go on."

I shrug and sit down, pull open the cellophane. "Since when do we get this stuff for breakfast, anyway? What happened to toast, and porridge?"

Mum smiles. "We'll have fish and chips later. Candyfloss."

"Can we?" Finn asks. "Really?"

"Yeah, course," Mum replies. "We're on holiday."

But we're not, I think to myself. We're not on holiday. This is it.

But thick dark chocolate coats the roof of my mouth

and sugar rushes to my head, dizzying, drowning the thought, trapping it in its stickiness. She's happy now, I think. Maybe that's all there is to it. The now. Not what happened all those years ago. Not what will happen tomorrow, in two months, three.

And I bite down again, flooding myself with sweetness and light.

Afterwards, Mum takes Finn to look at the sea. I say it's too wet out. But really I'm scared of being disappointed. Scared the Atlantic won't measure up to Cass's turquoise-water-and-white-sand photographs. Instead I wash up. It was fine at home, leaving dirty dishes for a day or two. But here it feels odd, like we're abusing someone, something. The house. Or Eleanor. I stack the plates back in the earth-damp cupboards, find a dish for the butter, a bin for the bread and the last of the pastries. Playing mother. I sing as I work, bits of stuff Luka played, CDs of Cass's; keeping myself company. It's not until I close the last cupboard door that I give in to the solitude and listen to the house. Its heaving silence, punctuated by the tick-tocking of the clock in the hall. Counting round the minutes in a place where time stands still.

I try to imagine Mum and Will running on this carpet, along these corridors. But I can't. This isn't a house for children. It's a grown-up place. All polished mahogany, watercolours, brass door handles. Proper. So different to London. There we lived in a kind of organized chaos: every wall a different shade of red, every shelf sagging under the weight of books, every sill crowded with clay models and cotton-reel dolls and plectrums. The flat was alive; it breathed with us, laughed with us. The walls here give nothing away. And I wonder if this suffocation that I feel is what Mum felt. And if that's why we lived as we did. Because she could breathe at last. Do what she wanted. Maybe I'll be different again. Minimalist or something. Mum says minimalists just have no imagination. But I think I'd like the space. The clean sharpness of corners.

My stomach swirls again; the insects are stretching their wings. Because I'm wondering now if Mr Garroway will repaint. Blot us out with two tins of magnolia. Like we were never there. Wondering if that's what Luka will find. Then I get this urge to phone home. Not the flat; I'm not that ghoulish, ringing to see if some stranger answers. But London, someone in London. Cass, I guess. Though she's probably out. Up the high street with Stella, or down Chicago's with Ash. Still, it's worth a try. I can leave a message, leave our new number. Then I realize I don't know our new number. Don't even know if there's a phone. I look around the drawing room – that's what Mum called it; not *living room*, because there's nothing alive about this place – but I can't see anything. No silver plastic cordless handset. Not even one of those retro ones with the dials. It's not in the kitchen either. Maybe there isn't one at all. Maybe they cut themselves off completely. An island.

The insects flap now, slow beats, but quickening.

I breathe harder, looking for something to calm them. And I find it. A flicker of memory of Luka with wire between his teeth and pliers in his hand. I go to the front door, and find what I'm looking for. Phone cable. Held against the frame in neat plastic keepers. No trailing wires to trip over here. I follow the line down and along the hallway skirting-board, trace its arc around the drawing-room door, then along the skirting again until it reaches its destination. An alcove. So small you might miss it at first. So dark it's hard to make out the tall circular table, the Yellow Pages and directory on a shelf at knee height. But it's there, and on the shining surface sits my treasure. A phone. Not cordless. But not old either. I pick up the receiver, half expecting it to be dead. But it isn't. Mum must have arranged it when she moved her benefits, changed the electricity and gas. Putting Luka down as well. Because even if she doesn't need his body in her bed, she needs his name for credit. The dialling tone buzzes in my ear like a thousand bees. I'm about to key in Cass's number when I notice the red light. Flicking on and off, on and off. Messages.

At first I wonder if it's Luka. If maybe Mum's passed the number on after all. But when I press PLAY I realize my mistake. They're not for Mum. They're for her mother.

There are two of them. The first, a woman, clear and clipped, reminding her about "Tuesday", hoping she hasn't forgotten, telling her to call back when she can. It could mean anything. A cup of tea. A bank raid. There are no other clues. No paper trail to reveal anything about her.

The second is different. A man's voice. Softer and tinged with West Country. And just one word. "Eleanor…" Then a click and dialling tone. But that word. It's a question, I think. "Eleanor?" Why just one word? And why didn't she erase the messages, I think, after she listened to them? Unless she left them for a reason. To remind herself. Or someone else.

But then it hits me. A hard shot, and true, straight to the stomach. I'm so stupid. She never listened to them because she couldn't. Because she was dead, crushed inside her car on a road miles from here. She never did call back about Tuesday. That man who said her name never heard her voice again. And I never heard it at all.

And I'm about to press DELETE when I remember something. If there are incoming messages, there must be an outgoing one. I press the button and pray to a God I don't believe in that it's not a generic American prerecord. I pray it's real.

It is real. It is her voice. Eleanor's. Cut-glass slicing through the cold air; I can almost see her breath. "I'm not able to answer the phone, but please leave a message, and I'll get back to you as soon as I can."

It says nothing. And everything. That she lived alone. That she was rich. Educated. Privately maybe, her voice a mix of BBC and royal. Then I'm struck by how weird this is. That she is talking to me from the grave. And I remember when Dion Clark died. This boy in our class at school who got hit by the Number 12 on Walworth Road. Cass kept a message from him on her mobile for weeks. She kept playing it again and again. Crying over it. Even though he'd only kissed her once then dumped her for Rae-Ann Jackson. Then her phone got nicked and he was gone and some other kid has a dead person on their voicemail now.

I press PLAY again. "I'm not able to answer the phone, but please leave a message, and I'll get back to you as soon as I can." And again. And again. This is her, I think. These are the only words I will ever hear her say. No telling me I've grown, no feigned shock at my outfits, no whispering she loves me. I press the button again. Addicted to the sound. To the sense of belonging and loss. I am so caught in it I miss the front door opening, the shaking of clothes, the kicking off of shoes. Before I have time to hide it, to press PAUSE, she's right there behind me. Her face is pale, set. And in an instant I know what she's going to do. But I still plead.

"Don't."

But she does. She clicks the buttons, all of them, again and again. Until the automatic American accent echoes along the hall, "Outgoing message deleted. All messages deleted." Then she pulls the wire out of the wall socket.

"We need some peace," she explains. "We're on holiday."

There it is again.

"Besides…" She shrugs. "Who's going to call us?"

Luka, I think. Nonno. Anyone. But I say nothing. Just wait for her to start humming again, to put the kettle on. Then I plug the phone back in.

HET

HET RINGS him late at night, when she knows her father will be asleep, and her mother too out of it to notice. Will is out. At Jonty's, or more likely drinking in the Golden Fleece. Leaning against the wall, legs stretching out catlike across the hallway, she talks softly into the receiver.

His brother Jimmy answers, laughs when he hears her whispered "Tom?" but fetches him anyway, both of them only just back from the fairground, working the waltzer and the win-a-goldfish stall. Real jobs, Het thinks. They're not the Gypsies Will calls them. Or worse.

She hears the phone clatter, words exchanged. "Tom?" she says again, hesitant this time.

But it is him. His voice hushed, too, though he has

no need; his mum gone, his dad in the pub gone closing every night. Maybe it's because of Jimmy being there. She knows what his brother thinks of her. That she is stuck-up. A student. Too good for them. Not like the town girls he goes with. Hair pulled back and tops pulled down.

"When can I see you?" he asks. "Can you come now?"

She shakes her head, forgetting he can't see her; her salt-dirty hair curling tendrils around her tanned face. Her longing.

"Het?"

"I can't," she says aloud. "Not tonight." Then pauses, thinks, decides. "Tomorrow. At the pier at ten."

"What'll you say?"

"I don't know," she admits. "Something. I'll think of something."

In the morning she tells her mother she is going to look for cowries.

Eleanor turns from her dressing-table mirror, eyelids heavy from the little white pills and rimmed with pink from crying. She looks at her daughter in the doorway. Nineteen years old, yet still lying like she did when she was nine. Keeping her skeletons, her secrets, buried inside. Eleanor wants so much to put her arms around her, to tell Het she knows where she's going, and who with. That she understands. That she's happy for her. But in her head she hears him. His measured words falling like fists, bruising her pale skin. That it cannot be allowed. That he will not be responsible for his actions if she condones it.

So instead she draws breath quickly, smiles and says, "That's nice, dear."

BILLE

THE HOUSE is full of secrets.

Over the next two days, the rain drums endlessly against the windows, its rhythm only breaking for the gusts of wind that blow it out to the sea for a few seconds before it comes back round to the glass again. Mum works out how to conjure up heat from the ancient boiler while Finn and I unearth things: a recorder, a felt kitten, a jar of cowrie shells. Mum smiles at them, at our delight in them, says, "Oh, that's from school … I made it … I collected them." But I can see the flicker in the corner of her eyes, the tightening of her jawbone, wincing, as though someone is pinching her slowly, secretly behind her back. And I am scared that this is just the tip of it. That somewhere in this house lies that Pandora's Box, full of things that will make her start with the pain of remembering.

I find it in the attic. Finn has begged and begged to be allowed up there, to dig around in the dust and cobwebs. Mum says, "Not now. Later." Repeats it like a mantra. Until in the end he gives in. But then so does she.

My timing is textbook. Finn is watching television, some programme that was forbidden at home. But not here, not on holiday. And Mum has lost something, an earring, is on all fours trying to find it in the thick green wool of the carpet. I say I'll be careful, that I won't touch anything that might break, that I'll watch where I put my feet.

"Fine," she says.

I shrug, not quite believing my luck but not saying another word in case she realizes what she's said, changes her mind.

The ladder slides down, attached to the loft floor by a pulley system so I can't get trapped. There is electricity too; a single bulb lights up the rafters. Wasps' nests cling to the beams, their paper intricacy intact despite the owners' long-since departure. But it is what lies beneath that draws out the gasp. I expected stacked boxes, the contents detailed in fat marker pen on the sides, shipping trunks, a rail of clothes. Even old furniture, a broken chair or a long-defunct cot. But instead there is a cavernous space, echoing with silence, and, under the spotlight of the bulb, a single unmarked box.

I am sure then, in that second, that this was left for me, the rest of the junk cleared out months ago, in readiness for this moment. This is it, I think, a skeleton in a closet, or in cardboard. Maybe a real one. I knew my grandfather had been a doctor, a surgeon, after all. But when I open it, I see not the creamy yellow-white of a rib-cage, of a Yorick skull, but soft red leather, edged in gilt. Not a skeleton, I think. Not bones. Photographs.

I flip slowly through the stiff vellum pages, peeling back the tracing-paper sheets in between to reveal the faces of this strange family, my family. At the table at Christmas, crackers held out in their hands, Will's pointing like a gun at the lens. It is only the second picture I have seen of him; the first, a cracked, faded thing in a drawer at home, his name and a date in blue-black ink on the back. A school photograph, his teenage years belied by spots, his tie loosened just enough to know that the sneer isn't an accident. A single memory, the others too painful, or too much to carry from here to London. Here he is a boy, seven or eight. Still playing cowboys and Indians, I guess. Or gangs, like Finn and his mates back in London, whooping round the street with lightsabres, until they see the real thing, or something like it.

There is one of Will and another boy, the same blond hair and ruddy cheeks as him, flushed with cold and flanking a snowman. It actually has a carrot for a nose, and a pipe. At home they wore bandanas, before the snow melted in the city fug and turned to dirty slush.

There is Mum. Aged five, aged fifteen, the same haunted look on her face. Not smiling; sullen.

And this must be Eleanor. Her mother. My grand-mother. She is beautiful, like Mum. But different too. Her hair straighter, swept back in a tight chignon, her face tighter. But her smile is as absent as Mum's. I see the lips move in my head, form the words I heard on the answerphone: the clipped accent, the crisp consonants. And I wonder what she said to Mum. To make her scowl. To make her leave. Or was it him?

There are just four photographs of the man I take to be her father; my grandfather. Two of him stiffly holding newborns; Will and Het. Then one of him in a surgical coat shaking hands with a man in a suit, both looking into the lens. A local newspaper kind of shot. I wonder if he'd won an award. Or retired. Yet he looks young still. His hair dark, his face unlined, yet severe.

I turn to the last page, to a family shot, all of them posed together, lined up on the lawn. Eleanor smiling, her husband's arm around her shoulder. Yet still she looks un-comfortable, strained. Next to her Will is pulling a face again, the collar of his rugby shirt turned up. Then Mum. Lost. Her face turned away, looking blankly at something in the distance, to the left of whoever was calling out "say cheese".

I look at the date underneath. It was taken the summer before I was born. I look hard at Mum's stomach but I can't see the trace of me yet. I wonder if she knows, if they know. If this is the last time they were all together. Before I came and put some unbreachable wall between them.

This isn't ephemera, I think. Not fleeting. Even though the bodies are gone, the bones buried or burned, the people are preserved. Captured in a single Kodak moment.

I close the album, its heavy binding snapping and sending motes of dust whirling in the beams of light. But then something bigger flutters down, a paper square, a Polaroid, twisting to the floor like a sycamore seed. It lands face up, and I start. Because this isn't a stranger. This is almost identical to a picture that was stuck to our fridge door with a magnet shaped like a cob of corn. Taken a second before, or a second after, its subject is the same. A fat-faced baby, mouth open, eyes tight shut, held in its mother's arms, her face chopped off by white edging.

This is a picture of me.

ELEANOR

"SMILE," SAYS Martha.

And Het does. Motherhood becomes her, she knows that. Even with the cracked sleep, the endless washing and drying and feeding, she shines somehow. The weight she felt before, the torpor, a ceaseless dragging at her chest, her legs, have gone. The midwife warned her about baby blues. Fussed about having family around to help, what with the father gone. Het shook her head. Said she didn't need them. That she had everyone she needed. Martha, and now Billie.

Billie chooses that moment to yawn. Martha laughs as she clicks the Polaroid shutter, jolts the camera, and the image spat out is missing part of its subject.

"Doesn't matter," says Het.

She holds the photograph between two fingers, fanning it back and forth to dry the ink. "No one wants to see me anyway."

Martha drops her head to one side, beseeching. "Come on, I'll take another."

Het groans. "She needs feeding."

Martha ignores her, holds the camera up anyway. "Say cheese," she says.

Het rolls her eyes, but obliges.

This time the photo is complete.

But this isn't the image that Het chooses. It is the cut-off photo that she will send. On the wide white strip underneath she writes her daughter's name and weight. No birth date. Because that would mean birthday cards and a knot in her stomach every year. So she picks her words carefully. Just enough so that they know she is real. And she is beautiful.

Eleanor recognizes the handwriting on the envelope. Has seen it morph from meticulously copied *as* and fat, open *b*s to the close, sloped script it is today. Her delicate fingers tremble as she slides the knife under the flap, pulls it sharply away. She hears the rip of paper, the clatter of the knife as she drops it onto the table, leaving a dent that cannot be polished out, that he will poke at later, worry over. But it is the *thud thud* of her heart that resonates loudest, and she is glad he is already out, worries the sound would betray her.

She slips her still-shaking fingers inside the brown paper

and takes out a single glossy rectangle. A burst of colour, of life, it hits her full square, knocks the breath out of her. Because now she knows she has lost not just a son and a daughter, but a granddaughter too.

She doesn't let him see it. Of course she can't. Instead the Polaroid hides in her handbag, thud thudding away, a still beating thing, reminding her, begging to be let out every time she fumbles for change or reaches for a lipstick. Then, one morning, in a burst of belief, of faith, of wanting, she knows who she can show it to. He will understand; will smile and hold her, tell her she should be proud, that she is a beautiful baby. With a beautiful grandmother.

She can see him through the gallery window. Sitting behind the wide wooden desk, his forehead creased, mouth drawn into an O as he studies a print held at arm's length. Eleanor touches her gloved hand to the handle of the door. But she cannot go in. Her belief has deserted her, drained away, and instead she scuttles back up the hill, ashamed, empty. The photograph she slips into the torn leather lining of an album, where he will never think to look, or want to. She knows this is the last of Het. That there will be no more pictures, no more envelopes. So she places the album in a box and carries it up to the attic. It will be safe there, she thinks. He won't find it. Then she lets the trapdoor slam shut, and gradually, in weeks, months, the thud of her tell-tale heart fades until all she can hear is the tick-tocking of the clock, and the screaming silence of what her world has become.

BILLIE

I WATCH Mum as she peels carrots at the sink. I haven't said anything to her about the photo. Because I don't know what words to use.

Cass used to say I wasn't missing anything, not having a nan, seeing as hers only ever sent her kids' stuff: kitten-covered cards and five pound book tokens. And anyway, I had Nonna. But now this is eating away at me. I wonder if he knew too. My dad. If there were three photos, three fat-faced baby Billies. If he had one, still has it maybe, taped to a fridge or hidden away.

It's raining again. An endless murky drizzle that seems to drip into your lungs, permeates your clothing until you can feel it trickle coldly down your skin. But I can't breathe in here any more. Need to get out. Need to start looking.

Mum looks up as I open the door. "Where are you going?"

"Just out," I snap at her, then regret it, wish I could swallow it back. It's not her fault, I think. She did what was best, she used to say. And I believe her.

Mum lets the words slide off her. "Be careful," she says.

I laugh, despite myself. I've done sixteen years in Peckham without getting shot. Or pregnant. What can happen here?

But Mum's not laughing. "Just. You know?"

I roll my eyes, pull my coat around me, a long wool Burberry, begged off Martha and finally relinquished in a fit of benevolence and bourbon. "I'll watch out for wolves," I say.

"You do that," she says. "No wolves."

"No wolves," I repeat.

But I forget about the sheep's clothing.

Seaton does what it says on the tin. The damp seems to have soaked into every surface, soaks into me as I trudge down the hill into town, collar turned up, a poor barrier against the mist of wet that runs rivulets down my neck. It has leeched the colour out of everything it has touched.

I study the pale faces that pass me, checking for... for what? My nose? My hair? I thought I'd recognize him. That there would be that light-bulb moment, that something would shift in me and I'd know that I was part of this person. But all I see are strangers. Grey-faced as the granite and pebbledash of the buildings, as the sea.

A flat, murky thing, half-hearted waves splutter onto muddy-looking sand. There are no deckchairs or donkeys here. A peeling sign on the rusting pier tells me the fairground is shuttered up until Easter. Yellow cellophane covers windows, shading out a non-existent sun, casting a sickly jaundiced glow on everything, on dead flies and Velvet Elvis pictures, china milkmaids. Only the palm trees remind me I'm in paradise: odd, airdropped things, so out of place I have to touch one to know it is real. Like me, I think. Airdropped exotica. Only I'm not: exotic, I mean. I pull my coat tighter around me, wishing I'd worn more. London got cold; colder even. And wet. But it was a different sort of rain. This kind drives into you, finds every seam; it even creeps into the lining of my boots so that my toes squeak damply with every step. I shiver and look around for somewhere warm, somewhere to wait in case the rain eases, though I know this is just wishful thinking.

I pass a row of arcades. I've been in places like them before. With Cass and Ash. Crowded round a fruit machine in Magic City, cheering and jeering at every nudge and hold. There they seemed like palaces, treasure troves; bright happy places, all fake crystal chandeliers and gilt-edged mirrors and the endless *chink chink* of coins clattering on metal. The promise of riches.

Here, a fat pasty-faced woman sits at a one-armed bandit, feeding coins from a plastic carrier bag while a toddler dressed as Tinkerbell leans, bored, against a pin-ball machine. The swirling carpet isn't thick and lush but worn and sticky with spilt soda. Spilt dreams. This isn't a palace. No chandeliers here. Instead neon strip lights just reveal a patina of grease and dust on the walls.

I keep walking, and next to a locked-up gallery is an Internet café, or an attempt at one. Two computers and a Coke machine squeezed into the back of a copy shop. I buy an orange Fanta and then hand another pound coin over to a greasy-haired man who points at one of the ageing Dells with nicotine-stained nail-bitten fingers. The fingers of the incurably addicted.

I check my email account and amongst the spam offers of Viagra and university degrees and hope is a single message from Cass.

Where's my bloody postcard, beeyatch? You won't believe what Ash has done now he's only gone and taken Stella up the Ministry of Sound and *blah blah blah*.

No "What's it like? How are you? Have you found him yet?"

I hit REPLY. Type in some stuff about the house, the rain. Saying nothing, like Cass, but taking four paragraphs to do it.

Then I click on Google.

I type in all I know. Two words and a number. *Tom, Seaton* and the year I was conceived.

I don't know what I was thinking. That somehow these three magic ingredients would work like a chemistry set, conjure up a picture, a name, a person? That somewhere in the ether he would be waiting for me to uncover him. But it's not enough. I need more clues. Need to know when he was born. Where he lived. God, I don't even know if he came from round here. I laugh at my idiocy, at the wild-goose chase of it all. And defeated, I log out.

I stand to leave, and the greasy-haired man looks up from his *Sun*.

"You've only had ten minutes," he says, his voice thick, clotted with cigarette tar, the vowels drawn out and lazy, like the cabbie's.

I shrug. "I'm done," I say.

He nods. "You on holiday?"

I shake my head. "No. It's just— I've moved. And the computer's not unpacked," I tell him, needing to explain my presence somehow, this pathetic figure. What I don't tell him is that the computer is broken after Mum threw a glass of water over the keyboard in one of her rages at Luka. And that I've barely got the money to pay for an hour of surfing, let alone a new hard drive.

He nods again.

I go to pull the door open, to let the wet in and myself out. But he stops me. He's holding something out in his yellow fingers.

"Here," he says. "Make up for the minutes you didn't use."

I take it from the chewed yellow fingers. It's a postcard. From a stand next to the counter. The picture is of Seaton. But not the one outside. This one is in Technicolor. The sea an impossible blue, crowds of sunbathers in decades-old outfits on sand the colour of custard.

"'S'not always raining," he says. "Send it home," he adds. "Make 'em jealous."

"This is home," I say to myself. Whether I find him or not, this is it now. I look at the cardboard paradise in my hand. And I hope he's right as I step out into the grey and the wet and the cold, cold town.

Het

IT IS May and Het is back in Cambridge. The air here is soft, light; breathing spring into the honey-coloured stone and still river backs. Hundreds of miles away from the stubborn wet of Seaton, the murky tides and the endless hammer of rain on the pier as they lie beneath it, arms and legs in a sand-coated tangle, lips touching and drinking each other in, filling each other with words and wonder at the newness of it, the realness.

Het finds the postcard in her pigeonhole outside the common room, sitting on a week's worth of rush-printed flyers for rave nights at the Junction and marches against the poll tax. The colours are acid-bright against the faded pastels, bleeding out onto her fingers. At first she thinks it's Will's idea of a *joke. Cheesy seventies postcard from home. "Wish you were here" and all that. Or her mother's, perhaps. Although she knows in either case it would be a lie. But then she turns it over.*

"Wish I was there," it reads. Four words and an x. A kiss, or to mark the spot.

But the writing is neither Will's nor Eleanor's. And Het finds her left hand clutching at the narrow wooden slots, as her heart races and her head dizzies with the thrill of it.

It is from him.

BILLIE

I'LL SEND it, I think. I'll send it to Cass. So she can laugh at the land that time forgot I've been transported to. But Cass doesn't care about stuff like that. She'd bin it like a fag packet or a screwed-up tissue. So I pick someone who does. I pick Luka.

There's a postbox across the street and I run out into the road, dodging a white Transit van. I forget this isn't Peckham High Street, an endless stream of buses, cars, lorries on their way to the West End and beyond. The van honks a reprimand and I mouth an apology. That would be something. Getting run over in a dead-end town.

The next post is at 11.15. I check my watch. 10.30. I don't have time to go home and get a pen. I fumble in the deep pockets of the Burberry but the lining is ripped in the left, and the right only turns up coins and a stick of Juicy Fruit. The postcard is getting damp, threatening to turn to mush. I need somewhere to borrow a pen, to sit and write it. I could go back to the Internet place but I don't want to talk to the nicotine man again. Besides, I need to find somewhere, a place that's mine. Like the Crossroads on Victoria Street. This old Italian greasy spoon. Cass and me would sit there, eking out one tea for hours. Laughing with Roberto at the builders on the Trivial Pursuit machine; watching the world, or Peckham, go by.

There's a restaurant, the Excelsior. Leatherette banquettes the colour of liver, and paper serviettes in dirty glasses. In the windows are faded photographs of food: steak and chips, a trifle, green-tinged now so they seem dusted with mould. I mentally cross it off a list, though they don't open until twelve anyway. Half the town is shut up. For the day, or for the season. I wonder where everyone goes. If they just sit it out behind their net curtains waiting for Easter and the tourists to start trickling in. Or if they've gone up to London, like Dick Whittington, like Mum, looking for streets paved with gold. And I'm pricked again by the thought that I've come here for this. For nothing. For rain and a boarded-up pier and empty shops. Nothing on the pavements but puddles and dog shit and gum. Same as everywhere.

I'm about to turn back up the hill when, on the corner, near the front, I hear the jangle of a door open, see a triangle of light shining on to the wet tarmac. A girl comes out. Fifteen, sixteen, dressed in the grey of a school uniform. Her hair a mass of pale curls glowing in the light behind. She lights a cigarette, smoke mingling with the fog of her breath as she huddles in the porch. Like Cass outside the Wishing Well. And I feel a rush of something – excitement, or relief. I walk towards her, towards the light and the heat and the dry. As I get closer I hear some indie band blaring out, low-slung guitars leaking under the doorframe; see blue tiles and a flash of red, and a sign. JEANIE'S. It's a café and it's open.

The girl pulls hard on her cigarette and looks me up and down, as if she's trying to add it up – the wet, lank hair, the coat, the boots. I smile, mumble a "Hi". She says nothing, just leans back to let me past, one eyebrow arched. She smells of cigarettes and too much perfume. The cheap stuff that comes in a spray can. As I push open the door she breathes out, letting smoke curl up through her hair. She is all that. And she knows it.

She follows me in, and I think for a minute she's going to trail me to the counter, flank me, demand to know who I am and what I want. But maybe I'm not worth it, because from the corner of my eye I see her blazered back head for a table, slump down in a plastic chair opposite a guy, older, but with the same eyes. Her brother, I guess.

The café is done out like some textbook seaside cliché. Red gingham tablecloths. Blue walls. But, like everything round here, it bears the signs of slow decay. The tiles are cracked, grime clinging to the grouting. The Formica tables propped on crumpled newspaper to keep them upright.

On top of the counter is a sponge cake; home-made. Underneath, juice cartons, Mars bars and millionaire's shortbread. God, I used to love that stuff. Begged Mum to bring it back from Martha's. Finn dancing around, happy that he was eating the same as a real millionaire, thinking somehow he'd be one now. The music blares from a CD system. I recognize it now. Kaiser Chiefs. It seems out of place here. Out of time.

I feel him before I see him. I'm still looking at the shortbread, wondering if I've got enough for a piece, for a slice of hope, when something shifts in the air and I hear someone coming out of the kitchen at the back, see a black shape appear behind the counter. Then I look up. And everything changes.

I wasn't looking for him. I wasn't looking for anyone like that. Mum always told me – even if I didn't tell myself – that I didn't need a boyfriend. Not yet. But maybe it was like the key again. Serendipity; fate. Even though I didn't believe in it.

I used to laugh at that stuff in magazines. Love at first sight. That your heart could stop. But I swear in that second everything stood still. The earth ceased turning and there was this sucking silence, draining everything around it, drawing the breath out of me. Then suddenly the world switched on again. The Kaiser Chiefs sang "Ruby", and I could hear the chink of china on china, smell bacon fat and coffee, feel my hand on cold glass. And him.

He was older. Eighteen, I guessed. Tall, taller than me. And this grace about him. But strength too, and confidence, without being arrogant. Like he knew who he was. Like he didn't care what anyone thought.

Maybe it wasn't fate. Maybe I'd willed this. Wanted this to happen. And he was just there at the right time. A coincidence. I'd waited at school. For a knight in shining armour who would ride in and rock my world, take me out of it. But all I got were kids like Ash and Leon, joking and smoking and giving it the big I am.

Yet now, here was a knight. And he didn't ride in. And he had long hair and a faded tour T-shirt instead of armour. But whatever, it happened.

"All right?" he says. "What can I get you?"

His voice is soft. The accent is there, but it's different on him. Makes him sound outdoorsy, a surfer.

I mumble back, still looking at the counter, unable to meet his eyes. I know I won't be able to eat shortbread. That it will stick in my throat, dry now from fear, or anticipation.

"Apple juice," I say. My voice is cracked. I cough and repeat it. Adding a "sorry". "And a pen," I say, remembering.

I reach into my pocket for change and dump a handful of coins on the counter before he can reach his hand out. Don't want to touch him, in case he can tell. A fifty pence piece rolls onto the floor and I feel my face redden.

"Sorry," I say again.

He laughs. "It's OK. Really."

I turn to glance at the girl. She's watching me, mouth open slightly, a smile on the edge of her lips, but not a friendly one. A crocodile smile. The kind that comes with a catch.

When I look back he's smiling, too. But this one is hiding nothing. This one is true. And it's meant for me.

"Here," he says.

In his hand is a juice box and a blue Bic biro. I hesitate, hoping he'll put them down, but instead he reaches further towards me. I hold my hand out and close it around the pen and carton. Our fingers touch for a second, and I feel it, a burning heat, like he's some storybook superhero. Except he's not; he's real. And in that instant I know, and when I meet his eyes, I see something there. A look that says he knows too.

I sit at the corner table. Away from the girl, my back to the counter. It takes me all of thirty seconds to drink the juice and scribble on the postcard. My new address. And our old one. The top-floor flat off the high street, with the broken-down boiler and the Blu-Tack stains and the F-I-N-N carved into the kitchen table when Mum wasn't looking. When I left the Internet café I thought I'd be funny, write, "Wish I was there." But in a few minutes everything has changed. I've changed. And instead I write, "Wish you were here."

Because I don't want to go back. Not even if I don't find my dad. Because I've found someone else. And I don't know his name. But I'm sure of it. That it's him, and always has been.

Het

THE FIRST time Het sees him is at the fair.

It is Easter and she is home from Cambridge to spend two clock-watching, tick-tocking weeks avoiding her father and ignoring her mother, bolting down her dinner so she can spend more time lying on her bed, refusing the pleas to get some fresh air, some exercise.

But the house is stifling. Her father boiling over some imagined slight on her mother's part. Will playing American rock so loud the bass notes reverberate through her. Het needs air. So she tells her mother she is going to the fair. Eleanor purses her lips, says isn't she too old? And besides, Jonty is coming for supper – doesn't she want to see him?

But Het doesn't. She wants candyfloss and coconuts and

goldfish in bags. She wants to fly. So at six o'clock she pulls her tangle of hair back into a ponytail and picks her old Crombie coat off the peg in the hall.

"Good God, you're not going out like that?" Her father stares in disbelief at this child in old man's clothing.

But she is going out like that. She bursts out of the door and runs down the hill, breathing in great gulps of briny air, feeling the sting of it on her face, its stickiness in her hair. Not caring that she will pay for this later. When she has to wash the sea from the heavy tweed before rot sets in. And endure the questions from her mother, and silence from him.

That night she rides rockets and eats a toffee apple, biting through the cracking cherry-red to the soft woody flesh beneath. Then, when she is done, she throws the stick carelessly onto a pile of polystyrene burger boxes, and climbs up onto the waltzers. Ignoring her mother in her head, telling her she'll be sick, that she always is.

That's when she sees him. Leaning over her as he clunks the safety barrier into place. Het looks up at the face just inches from hers and sees something, some trace element, a mineral she knows she needs, that she has been waiting for. She opens her mouth to speak, but instead he kisses her. Right then, before he's even said a word to her, before he even knows her name, he leans in and pushes his mouth onto her toffee-apple lips. He tastes of cigarettes and peppermint and life.

"What are you doing?" she says when he pulls away.

"Something," he laughs. "Everything."

And instead of heavy shame, she feels weightless. And she knows in that instant it is him.

BILLIE

BUT, JUST like that, like a superhero, like a knight, he's gone. I sit in the café for two mornings straight, clasping a cracked mug of cold tea; scum clinging to its surface, I've made it last so long. Behind the counter is a woman, older, hair scraped back in a thin ponytail, gold earrings and necklaces like she's 50 Cent. The music's changed too. Mariah Carey and Beyoncé. Like it's a different place. I wonder if I made him up.

I figure I should forget it. Can't keep waiting. Like a stalker, a sad case.

Besides, I have to visit my new school, meet the head-teacher. Finn has seen his already, St Mary's Primary, full of toilet-roll puppets, and murals of tigers, and guinea pigs in a cage. He wants to start now so he can paint wild animals, hold the guinea pigs, but the headmistress says he's to wait until after Easter; it'll be easier then. She's set him a project, something to do with the Tudors. Mum is delighted, says his old school would never have done that. Says it shows how right she was, how right we were, to move away.

Mum wants to come with me too, to see the new-computers-and-no-graffiti of her imagination. More evidence for her. But I fob her off, say I'd rather go alone, tell her it's about independence. And anyway, Finn needs her to do stuff on Henry VIII.

She'd be disappointed anyway. Seaton High isn't bright and shiny and new. It's old, and dirty. A great draughty Victorian thing, the walls glossed in wipe-clean Starburst orange and green. Like Peckham Park was before they knocked it down and built the Academy, as if shiny chrome and glass and new carpet would change everything. Still the same teachers, the same kids from the same estates. Same dealers at the gates. And within a month the chrome and glass is sticky with hand prints and the carpet stained with Coke and spit and blood.

I'm not fooling myself like Mum. School is school, and it'll be the same here as it was there, as it is everywhere. Only this one is here. In his town. Near him.

I sit in the corridor outside the headmaster's office, on a plastic chair with gum stuck to the underside and *Dane* carved into the back. Kids stream past talking about last night's TV and tomorrow's footie; voices hushing when they see me, then whispering behind folders covered in stickers and cartoons and *Lianne* ❤ *Justin*. Then the bell rings, and they disappear, like a shoal of fish, scattering through open doorways, flickers of uniform blue. Then I'm alone in the Dulux orange glow again.

I'm still waiting when I hear someone slump into the chair next to mine; smell too much perfume and cigarettes, and mint to cover them, failing to hide a dirty habit. I turn to say something, hello, I guess, but I see who it is, see the tight curls, and that smile, that sneer.

"I know you," she says.

I don't reply. Not sure what I'm supposed to say.

"You were in the café. Where you from? Truro?"

I shake my head. "London."

"My cousin lives in London. Shona. In Wood Green."

She looks at me, waiting. In case I know her.

I shrug. "It's kind of a big place."

"Like, duh." She takes the gum out of her mouth and sticks it under her chair.

I smile and she shoots me a look.

"How come you moved here then? It's a hole. Should have stayed in London."

"It's … complicated," I say finally. "My mum grew up here. We inherited a house." For a second I think about mentioning my dad. But what would I say? That I'm looking for a man called Tom who could be anything from thirty to ninety for all I know, and who might, just might, have come from round here. It'd make me sound desperate. Crazy, even. So instead I just add, "Whatever." Like it balances it out. The thought. The childish thought.

"So, you know anyone?" She twists a curl slowly round a bitten-nail, chipped-varnish finger, lets it spring back.

"No."

She thinks about this. And for a minute I think she's looking at me like Cass used to look at half the girls at the Academy. Like I'm sad, Billy-No-Mates. And that she'll dismiss me like Cass did them, flick fag ash on me. But instead she says, "Wanna meet us down the Clipper later?"

I start, then hide it. Affect disinterest. Playing the game. "Who's us?"

"Me. Jake – that's my brother. His flatmate."

I shrug. "Maybe. I don't know." Don't know what Mum will say. Where I'll get the money.

"Well, whatever," she echoes. "We'll be there at eight."

I nod.

"Billie Paradise?"

We both look up. A woman, the secretary, is standing in the doorway, waiting for me.

"Yeah," I say, standing. I turn to the girl. "See you."

"Wouldn't want to be you," she says.

Something Cass would say, and I smile, say, "You wouldn't."

"Not with a name like that."

I pull up my bag and walk towards the office.

"Eva," she calls after me.

I turn back.

"That's my name. Not that you even bothered to ask."

"Eva," I repeat.

She nods, and then unwraps another stick of Double-mint, drops the paper in her bag and goes back to radiating boredom.

The headmaster is Mr Gold. Fifty-something and still thinking he's seizing the day and changing the world.

"These are good results, Billie." He leafs through the forms in front of him, exam results and reports sent on from the Academy. "So, what is it you want to do?"

I'm not sure what he means. "A levels?" I try.

He laughs. "I know that. I've got it here. Art, English and History. That's all fine. What I mean is: what do you want to do with your life?"

I look blankly back at him. He tries again.

"Who do you want to be, Billie?"

I look to the ceiling for inspiration, find nothing but a metre-long crack, and end up saying what I always say. "I like drawing. And I'm good... At least my old teacher thought I was."

He nods. "So, a budding Damien Hirst, then?"

The stock answer. Never mind that he's a charlatan, or so Martha says. Because he got everyone else to paint his dots for him.

But I say, "Yeah." Because it's easier that way.

When I get out Eva has gone. Done a bunk. Like Cass would have. And I smile. Because school is school. Whether it's chrome and glass or peeling orange. Even the kids are the same.

HET

HET WROTE home from Cambridge every fortnight in her first term, just as Eleanor had asked. Long letters about the punts and the pale honey-stone and how odd the traditions seemed, gowns at dinner, tea with the bursar. She described her room in painstaking detail, the latticed glass and wood-panelled walls. Wrote stories of the other girls on her floor, how they had joined the Film Society and the Lacrosse Club, and that Anna in 3B was already in Footlights.

What she didn't tell them was that she never went with them. That she didn't want to see films or play lacrosse or meet boys in dusty rehearsal rooms. That she loathed the girls and boys in equal measure. The girls were too earnest and determined. And the boys reminded her of Will and Jonty, full *of themselves, and fat bottles of Chardonnay, and the knowledge that they would inherit the earth.*

She didn't tell them that every time she picked up a book the letters blurred in front of her and her mind shut like the snap of a vanity case.

That it all seemed so pointless.

That instead, she wandered the Backs. Sat by the Cam, or in Belinda's, with a cold cup of tea and a paperback. That's where she met Martha: wiping down tables and pouring coffee with her first in Classics. Saving up to move to London, to find fame and fortune, or at least a job somewhere better than this.

And Martha took pity on her, this Cornish girl with the wild hair, and pale eyes, and the copy of Middlemarch *that she never seemed to finish.*

So it was Martha who she told about Tom. Martha who knew about the pregnancy. And it would be Martha who she ran to that night she left for good.

"Will you ever go back?" Martha asks one night, weeks later.

Het shakes her head quickly. "No." But then she catches a memory, a fleeting thing, like a butterfly in a net. A memory of the sea, and the sand, and the sun. And of him. "Maybe," she adds. "When they're gone."

"Who?" asks Martha. "When who is gone?"

Het looks up, frowns, as if it's obvious. "The ghosts."

BILLIE

MUM IS cooking when I get back. Something with red wine that sizzles and spits at her as she pours it into the pan; the rest of it into a finger-printed glass on the counter, filled and drained once already.

"I rang the solicitors," she says. "Asked where the rest of Eleanor's money was, because it can't have just gone, and it's yours really. But they wouldn't tell me."

She takes a swig from the glass, stirs the pan. "Can you believe it? I mean, I'm family. And they wouldn't tell me. You should ring. They'd tell you. I bet they would."

"I don't think so," I say. "They're not allowed. You know, confidentiality."

But even I'm wondering. Because there must have

been money. He was a surgeon. And it can't all have been used up settling bills. So where did it go?

"Oh my God." Mum turns. "School. How was it?"

"Oh. Fine. You know, school-like."

"Have they got guinea pigs?" Finn asks. "Mine's got guinea pigs."

"No," I say. "At least, I don't think so."

"Never mind," says Mum, ignoring the fact that I don't even like the things. "I'm sure it will be perfect. Once you've made some friends."

Then I remember.

"I met someone," I say. "Eva. A girl." Like it's not obvious.

Mum whirls, wine sloshing down her hand, dripping onto the floor. "What's she like? How old is she?"

"Fifteen, I think. Not sixth form. Year Eleven."

I realize I'm not sure of anything about her. Except her name.

"That's great," Mum says. She's happy. Billie's-got-a-friend, half-a-bottle-of-red happy.

So I push my luck. "She's asked me to meet her. Tonight."

"Where?" asks Mum through the rim of the glass.

"Can I come?" asks Finn.

"No. At the Clipper. It's a pub, I think."

"No way," says Finn. "You never let her go to the pub," he points out to Mum.

But this is different. This is here. And now.

"Well, you'll need some money," she says finally. She puts down the glass and reaches into a coffee jar, pulling out a tenner.

"What's that?" I ask.

"Emergency funds," Mum says. "They didn't think to take that. Ha!"

"Where was it?"

"Where it always was." She picks up her glass again, takes a swig. "In the cupboard."

But when I get to the pub, she's not there.

I sit in the corner with my drink. Being tall counts for something; the barman didn't skip a beat, just poured the vodka into a glass with a dried-up slice of lemon and thumped the Schweppes bottle down next to it.

I was expecting some country inn, like you see on TV. All bare wood and log-fire warmth. The place is warm, at least: a gas fire is lit; three bars glow blue-orange in a copper surround. The rest is no different to the Wishing Well that Mum thinks I stayed out of. Foreign notes stuck on the ceiling with drawing pins, a quiz machine and a jukebox blaring out Status Quo.

I look at my watch. Half eight. Bitch, I think. She's probably outside with some skanky friend. Waiting till I leave so she can laugh and point and prove I'm nothing, nobody. I stir my drink with the straw, releasing tiny cells of lemon flesh to cloud the neon.

"All right?"

I look up, and hate myself. Because it's her.

"Eva."

"We were waiting for Mercy." She flicks her eyes to the bar, to a girl with long auburn hair, her arm snaking around Jake's back.

"Right. His flatmate," I say.

She laughs, a short harsh sound. "You're joking. She wouldn't live with him." She flips a beer mat, looks up. "This is his flatmate."

And I feel it again. That second of heart-stopping silence. Because I know who's behind me before I turn. See the black T-shirt reflected in Eva's eyes.

It's the boy from the café.

I don't want to look up. In case I'm wrong. In case I'm right. Don't know which is worse. But I don't need to. Because he sits down next to me. And Eva's smile twists into that sneer again.

"Billie Paradise – meet Danny Jones. Danny – meet Billie. Oh, wait. You already know each other."

"No, I—" I stutter.

"The café," he says. His voice soft, like cotton wool holding me.

"No— I remember... It's just... I don't, you know, *know* you."

Eva snorts. And I wonder then if he is hers. Or if she wants him to be. If he does. But he sat next to me. *Me*.

I close my fingers tight around my glass. Down it quickly, the heat burning my throat, making me cough.

"Want another?" Danny asks.

"Yes— No. I mean, I can't buy a round." I feel my cheeks flush with shame and alcohol. I've only a fiver left and some change. What an idiot.

"It's OK. I'm a working man. Besides, it's Jake's round," he smiles, his eyes waiting for a yes.

I give him one. "Vodka and tonic." Like I drink it every night. Like I'm Cass, with her jelly shots and Bacardi Breezers and throwing up on the Grove so she can walk in the door sober.

But Eva knows different. "How old are you?"

"Seventeen. Nearly." Old enough, I think. Older than you.

But Danny's gone. And then there's another vodka in front of me, cold and sweet and lemon-soaked. And he's squeezing up next to me to let Jake and Mercy in. And Jake makes some joke and even Eva laughs and then it doesn't matter any more if I'm sixteen, or eighteen, or whatever.

"Cheers," someone says.

"Cheers." I smile. And I mean it.

We stay until closing, until last orders and time have been rung. Until there are four empty glasses in front of me and four hundred "Remember whens" and "This girl at school" and "Mikey said Jonny said". In return I've told them about London. About the time Cass got burgled when she was in bed, about the gun Leon's brother Ray has under his mattress. Showing off. Vodka pulling the words out of me, blurring the edges, making it easier for me to look at him. To know he's looking at me. Then I tell them about Mum and Finn and the house. About Luka and the tour. Hear Eva say, "Is he your dad and all?" Hear me reply, "Kind of. As good as."

By the time we burst out of the gas-fire glow onto the empty street I am drunk. Eva pushes her arm through mine, and I let her, this stranger.

"The pier," she says.

"Yes, the pier," I say, like I've been there a thousand times. Like it's filled with memories for me too.

We walk. Or stagger. Eva's arm still locked in mine, Danny behind me, laughing with Jake about something I don't hear and wouldn't get anyway.

We push and dance our way along the jutting iron, our erratic steps echoing off wooden planks as we pass the shuttered fairground: the donkey derby, a carousel, a rocket ride and the waltzers. Past candyfloss cabins and hot-dog stalls. All shuttered, still. It's eerie, I think. The stuff of horror films. Of nightmares. But I'm still laughing. Then we get to the end.

We're in a line, leaning over the thin railing, breathless, staring into the black water below. It's bottomless. The only movement a slow slosh against the rusting legs.

"Anyone for a swim?"

Jake is standing on the bottom rung, arms wide like he's on the bow of the *Titanic*. Without warning, he grabs my arm and pulls me up with him. I see the water below me, feel the sudden lurch of fear. Feel the insects that have lurked in my stomach all night scatter. Suddenly I'm sober. Scared.

"No." I wrestle his arm, try to shake him off. Then louder, "No. I can't. I can't swim."

I hear Mercy shout his name, but he's still holding me and I lash out in panic, sobs rising in my throat. Then I feel another arm grabbing me, pulling me down, back onto the boardwalk, back to safety. Danny.

"You OK?" he asks. I nod, quickly wiping the eyes that betray me. Don't want him to think I'm like this.

His hands drop away and I will them back, but instead, he turns to Jake. "Idiot."

"Joke," Jake protests. "Jesus."

"Don't worry about it, Billie," Mercy says. "He wouldn't have. No one swims here. Not any more."

I look down again. And I don't get it. Because even though I wouldn't, couldn't, the water looks like silk, its blackness somehow inviting. "Why not?"

"Undertow," Eva says. "It's this kind of, I don't know, secret pull. The water looks still on the surface, but underneath there's a current, dragging everything out to sea."

"Aren't you supposed to swim sideways or something?" I say, remembering a TV news report.

Eva snorts. I guess not.

"It pulls you under," Jake says. "If you fight it you just drown quicker."

"Drown?"

"Yeah," says Eva, eyes wide with mocking. "The sea-bed's littered with skeletons. It's like *Pirates of the Caribbean* down there. Davy Jones's Locker."

"It's not a joke," Danny retorts. "What about that kid last summer?" He turns to me. "This boy fell in and went under, then his dad jumped in to get him. They both drowned."

I shiver. The last traces of vodka heat have drained away, and the rain has started again, a steady drumming, sticking my hair to my face.

"Come on." Danny tugs at my arm. "I'll walk you home."

I feel a rush of nausea, of anticipation, and I don't know if I'm glad or angry when Eva springs up from the railing.

"I'll come."

Danny laughs. "Don't be stupid, you live in the opposite direction."

"So?" She is determined.

"It's fine," I say. And part of me thinks it is, that I want her to come. Scared in case he tries anything. Scared in case he doesn't. But I'm outranked.

"No it isn't," Jake says. "Who's going to walk you home, Eva?"

"Danny," she says.

"Thanks." Danny rolls his eyes.

"I'll walk myself then."

"Nope, you can come with me and Mercy." Jake pulls her towards him, nods at Danny, like he's doing him a favour. "See you, Billie." He grins at me now. "Good to meet you."

"Yeah," I say. Then, "Good to meet you too I mean."
Shit.

Eva rolls her eyes. "See you around."

And then they're gone, their backs disappearing behind the wooden slats of a stall. And it's just us. Me and Danny.

Alone.

We walk up Camborne Hill in silence, a handspan between us, centimetres that crackle with possibility. But Danny's hands are deep in his pockets, mine clasped round me, hugging my rain-heavy coat tight against the cold, trying to contain the insects that are in me again, flapping their wings in fear and excitement.

We reach the top and I feel my stomach tighten. Do I ask him in? What if Mum's up?

But when we get to the gate I can see the stained-glass of the door is dulled to murky browns. The lights are out. They're in bed.

"This is it," I say.

"Nice house," he says.

I shrug. "It's kind of old, inside. Old person." I stare down at the tiles, trying to find courage in the tight tessellation. "So—"

"Did you mean it?" he interrupts.

I look up. "What?"

His eyes are on me, in me. "About not swimming?"

I drop my head again. "Yeah," I say quietly. Like an apology. Because it is. Because I'm this no-clue city girl, and he, he must be born to it. Him and Jake and Mercy and Eva, all of them. And it's not like it's a fear or anything – not like Mum, who shivers at the thought. Just that she never took me, and school, well there's other stuff to learn in Peckham. Swimming's not really a survival skill there.

"I could teach you," he says.

"What?" I blurt, shocked.

He's defensive. "No. Sorry, bad idea. You should get lessons—"

"No, that would be great. Thanks." God, what am I saying?

"Oh. Right. I'll check out the pool, find a good time."

"Cool," I say, not knowing if I mean it or not.

"Cool," he repeats.

Then the silence is back, the crackling gulf. I should say it now, I think. Ask him if he wants a cup of coffee. But the courage I found on the tiles is gone. The words won't come out. Not now. Not tonight. Instead I push my key into the lock, turn the handle.

"I should—"

"Right, yeah." He comes to.

"Thanks for walking me home," I say.

"Any time."

"Night, then."

He nods. "Night." Then he turns and is gone.

I shut the door behind me and lean against the wall, my breath coming in short gasps. I'm laughing. I clap my hand over my mouth to cut off the sound. Don't want to wake anyone. But then I see it, a rectangle of pale green spreading across the carpet, the tell-tale fluorescent glow leaking out from under an ill-fitting door. I was wrong; someone is up.

She's in the kitchen, sitting at the table, surrounded by our dinner plates congealing with the last of the spaghetti bolognese, staring at a big fat nothing on the wall.

"Mum?" I say.

But if she hears me she doesn't show it. Ears and mouth muffled by the wine, I think.

I wonder if she's been sitting there all night. Nothing's moved since I left, it seems, just Finn, gone to bed. But then I see something else in the sea of dirty plates and glasses. A glint. Treasure.

I reach down and pick it up. It's a silver chain, a locket. Not hers. Or mine. I open my mouth again to ask her where she found it, whose it is, but I feel a dizzy rush, realize I'm going to be sick, and instead I drop the locket, turn and run.

I hunch over the toilet bowl, but nothing comes up. Why should it? Only four vodkas, I think. Cass could do nine before she puked. My eyes and stomach ache from the heaving though. So I flush and, ignoring my toothbrush, walk slowly back along the corridor to Mum's old room, wrap myself in the covers, and sink into sleep, a rabbit in my hand, and Danny in my head.

HET

AN EIGHT-YEAR-OLD *Het eyes the silver thing in her mother's fingers. The thin chain hanging like a single thread of cotton, and, clutched in her palm, the pendant, a cold, hard metal lozenge. Open and shut she flips it, open and shut. Each time ending with a satisfying click.*

It is seven in the evening and Het is lying on her parents' bed, chin resting in her hands, watching as her mother goes through the motions of getting ready. The Pan-Stik, powder and rouge. The thick pink grease on her lips and black smudges on her eyelashes. The droplets of Chanel that drift gently to the floor like a perfumed curtain call, signalling that she's done. Ready. For something Het longs for and dreads at once. Parties and people and life.

Tonight it is cheese and wine at the Listers'. Jonty's parents. Het has heard them argue about it. Her mother says she is tired. That she would rather stay at home with the children. But her father dismisses this, brushing it off like a speck of lint on his suit sleeve, says the girl will be here to babysit any minute and she must change into something more suitable, or does she intend to wear trousers to a party? As if it would be a crime so great she might be punished infinitely. So Eleanor drifts up the stairs, Het trailing her like a shadow.

Eleanor holds the chain up to her throat, drapes it around her pale skin.

"Het?" she says. "Can you…?"

Het drops her bare feet to the carpet, stands and takes the gossamer metal in her hands. The fastening is tiny, and her fingers struggle with it, her thumb straining to hold the clasp open while she feeds the loop through. Het can feel her mother's breath quickening, her limbs tensing, but finally it is done, and she releases the clip with a gasp.

Her eyes meet her mother's in the mirror, and for a fleeting second there is a connection, an understanding. But then the door rattles in its casing and he is there, stiff in his blazer and grey wool trousers. His face reddened with port and effort. And Het shrinks back to the sanctuary of the bed, draws her knees up tight and holds them, making herself small, so small he won't see her.

"Where did you get that?" he says.

His voice isn't raised, but Het can hear the anger. Each

word measured, calculated to dig in, to hurt just so much.

"I— I'm sorry. I wasn't thinking…"

"You never do," he replies.

"I…" Eleanor trails off. His hand is at her throat now; he grasps the necklace in his surgeon's fingers, pulls it sharply, precisely. Het sees it dig into whitening skin, threatening to strangle her, to slice into flesh. But the metal is too fragile; the links give way and it snaps, the locket falling soundlessly onto the floor, the chain following as he drops it like a dirty swab, wipes his hand on the blue flap of his jacket.

"Five minutes," he says, then he turns and walks out, his tread steady on the stairs, trailing fury in his wake.

Het lets a sob escape and Eleanor turns in shock. She had forgotten her, forgotten this witness.

"Oh Het…" She reaches a hand out, wants to pull the child into her lap, to tell her it is all right. But then she hears his words again, cutting through her like a knife into butter. She lets her hand drop and turns back to her reflection, forcing her lips into a wide coral-coloured smile. "That's enough, darling. It was just an accident. Mummy will wear the pearls instead. Now run along, the babysitter is here. If you're a good girl she might let you watch telly."

Het wipes salty snot on the back of her hand, then bolts from the room. But she doesn't go downstairs. Instead she runs to her bed, slides between the mattress and bedsprings. Lets the heavy foam and flannelled bulk pin her down, the iron coils dig into her back.

* * *

When she comes out it is dark. Het tiptoes along the corridor to her parents' room. She opens the drawer in the vanity mirror, searches the sage carpet with her fingers, feeling for the hard metal. But the locket is gone.

BILLIE

IT'S LATE when I wake up, gone breakfast. Yet my limbs are still heavy with sleep, aching, pinning me to the mattress. For a few seconds I think I'm ill, that the endless rain and cold has leached into my bones, filling me with flu. But then I see my clothes in a heap on the floor, feel the last drops of vodka in my stomach, an acid sting, and I remember. Remember the way his smile plays on the corners of his mouth then broadens into a slow, lazy grin. Remember his eyes, treacle-dark. Remember the way I look reflected in them, standing on the doorstep, wondering, waiting for what might happen next.

But then the picture in my head changes, and I see something else. Someone else. Mum, sitting at the table, entranced, lost. And the warm milk sweetness goes cold and curdles.

When I get downstairs the drawing room is a war zone. The polished mahogany lost under a haphazard pile of china ornaments and dust-heavy leather-bound books. Finn is going through a box of cutlery, silver set against navy velvet, counting forks and spoons, like Fagin in his slum. And in the middle of it all is Mum, eyes wide and wild, surveying the chaos.

"What's going on?" I ask quietly.

Mum swings around, eyes narrowing to see who has interrupted her, then smiles when it is me. "I'm having a clear-out." The words are hammered out, fast, like shots. She is speeding, racing. "Isn't it marvellous? Look at it all."

I look. At the *Wisden Almanack*s. The watercolours. Will's trophies, stacked carelessly in a cardboard box. All that achievement tossed aside. Because, what? Because they loved him more? Because he died, leaving her alone with them?

And something else. On the table, chain dangling over the side, is the locket. I pick it up, let the delicate links tumble through my fingers, then click it open to see who is inside.

An oval photograph. A boy's face. Blond hair and ruddy cheeks. Will. But where is Mum?

"Where did you get it?" I ask.

Mum snatches it out of my hand. "Nowhere. Doesn't matter."

She snaps the locket shut, looks at it in her palm. "The chain's broken, but it's silver. Still worth something. I'm going to sell it on eBay."

"We don't have a computer." I state the obvious, though I know she'll have an answer. She always does.

"I'll call an antique dealer then. They'll take the good stuff. The rest can go to a charity shop. We need some space. Light. It's too cluttered in here. Don't you think, Billie? Too cluttered."

I want to tell her it's mine, really. That I should get to decide. But I can see something in her. Not wine this time. Nothing she's taken. But something that's missing. She's going. Slipping under. I can feel it.

So instead, I nod my answer. But she's not even looking. She's gone, to find a man who will take away all this junk, this treasure. This ephemera. Take away the lives of others so she can start living again.

The dealer comes later that afternoon. Kenneth Shovel: Call-Me-Ken. He has dandruff on the collar of his brown nylon suit. He says it's not worth that much any more, silver. Just what he can get for scrap. But he'll give her two hundred pounds for the trophies and one of the paintings. A watercolour of the beach by no one I've ever heard of. Mum drops the worthless locket in a charity bag and takes the crisp notes like she's been handed two hundred thousand. And Call-Me-Ken drives off in his white Transit with a smile like Simon Cowell and the bargain of the century.

"We should celebrate," Mum says.

I watch as Finn counts the notes, recounts, assessing our fortune. Two hundred pounds. It's nothing. Not really. A few weeks' shopping. Or a few days'.

"We could save some," I suggest. "In case."

"In case what?" Mum is fidgeting.

"I don't know." Don't want to say it: because you don't have a job, because benefits never pay all the bills.

"Well then." Mum has won. "What shall we do? The world is our oyster."

"I'm hungry," says Finn.

"Dinner. Perfect," says Mum, kissing him on the top of his head. "My boy genius."

Then she turns to me, waiting for the chorus of disapproval. But I can't. Can't tip the fine balance.

"We could get fish and chips," I say.

But it's no good. Mum doesn't want fish and chips. She wants liver-coloured leatherette and napkins in glasses and steak and Knickerbocker Glories. She wants the Excelsior.

"We're rich," she laughs. "Millionaires."

"Are we really?" asks Finn, his chin shiny and bright with chocolate sauce and hundreds and thousands.

"No," I should say. "We're not. Not really. We're broke. With a draughty house that will leak money like it leaks heat."

But I'm high on ice cream. On hope. Like Mum. So I lie for her.

"Almost," I say.

And even though dinner costs more than fifty pounds. Even though Mum spends another tenner on the way home buying more wine. Even though Finn is sick in the night, a Knickerbocker stream of indulgence flushed away. For that moment, reflected in Mum's eyes, we are. We are almost millionaires.

Het

TOM IS *everything Jonty isn't. Not just his height; his build: tall and lean rather than rugby-solid. But the way he is with her. The way he holds her, the way he talks to her like she matters, like she's all that matters. Not like Jonty's braying monologues. Where Het gets the feeling he's just enjoying the sound of his own voice. Tom listens, too. Listens to her tell him about college. About how she doesn't fit. Never has.*

Het hears Will's voice, reasoning with her: "He's just not one of us, Het." And he isn't. But he's not what Will thinks he is either. One of them. A no-good Gypsy. Not like Jimmy, with a girlfriend and a kid and a string of women. Tom belongs to nobody. Like her.

* * *

He takes her out to dinner. To the Excelsior. He heads for a booth at the back but she pulls him to the window, where they can see, and be seen. The seat is the colour of blood. Leather, or vinyl probably, her bare legs sticking to the surface, sweaty with excitement and the heat of July.

She can barely finish her steak, chewing each mouthful until it is nothing but gristle, her mouth too dry to swallow. But he orders dessert anyway, if only to show he can. The waiter brings a Knickerbocker Glory. An absurd thing, she thinks. A show-off pudding. He feeds her from a long silver spoon, cream and a cherry, a taste of sugar and boiled sweets. She shakes her head at another and watches him instead, eating this beautiful thing, this work of art, until there is nothing left but a tiny pool of molten vanilla.

Dinner costs twenty-five pounds. A weekend's wages from the fair. But it is worth it. She is worth it.

"Next time it's my treat," she tells him.

He shakes his head but she insists. And on Saturday she takes him for fish and chips, eaten out of the vinegar-soaked newspaper on the seafront. It is perfect. Like him.

BILLIE

THE NEXT day Mum goes out and spends a hundred and fifty pounds in two hours. On what, I don't know. A new camera. DVDs for Finn. Food; bags of two pound-a-go rocket that will lurk in the fridge until they melt into inedible brown slime. Instead of pasta, we have high tea. Every meal an elaborate display of shop-bought cupcakes, quails' eggs already peeled, sausages on sticks, jam sandwiches cut into heart shapes like I'm a princess. Or a kid. Like Mum is a kid. It's like when Cass's dad first went to live with her step-monster and every day Cass had chips for tea. Chips with everything, like they could make it all better. Only they didn't. Cass got so sick of them she said she could taste them in her mouth if anyone even said the word.

At the end of the week, Mum puts a plate of cheese straws down on the table for breakfast and I can't stand it any more. We need money.

"I'm going out," I say.

I don't tell her where. Won't until I get back, until I've got something. It'll be easy, I tell myself. Resort towns are full of jobs. Cleaners and waitresses. And I walk down the hill, ignoring the weather, and the shuttered windows and every other reminder that this isn't Brighton or Blackpool, and it isn't high season.

The Grand is a joke. Maybe once upon a time it lived up to its name. But now its paint is peeling, the red nylon carpets worn and stained. Brass lamps give everything a seedy glow. It is tatty, tawdry, faded. But I figure at least the cleaning should be easy. I mean, it's not like they'll sack me for missing a bit. I put on my I'm-totally-reliable-and-don't-ever-do-drugs face and walk up to the desk. The receptionist is older, and fat, her breasts squeezed into a too-small bra under a shiny satin shirt.

"Hi. I'm looking for work."

She raises a fat boiled-egg eye from her *Chat* magazine but doesn't say a word. I try harder.

"Cleaning, or, um, waitressing?"

"We're empty. Try at Whitsun."

"Oh." I do my winning smile and am about to ask for a pen and paper to leave my name and address when I realize she's not even looking at me any more, she's gone back to Kelly-from-Harlow's true confession.

It's the same at the Palace, and the row of seedy B&Bs on the main road. Laughing, raised eyebrows and "Come back in a few months". But I don't have a few months.

In the window of the Excelsior is a handwritten ad for a sous-chef. I don't even know what a sous-chef is but I figure the hours will be OK because restaurants don't really open until after school. But the owner, his accent slipping from Cornetto ad Italian to broad Cornish, tells me I need experience; it's not McDonald's. I look at the pictures of the green meals. It so isn't, I think. And for once I find myself wishing it was. That I was back in Peck-ham, under the Golden Arches. Anyone could get a job there. Even Ash, for a few weeks anyway. Before he started nicking stuff.

"You could try Jeanie's."

I come to. "What?"

"The caff." He nods down the road to the seafront.

There it is. The cracked-tiled, red-gingham, Danny-full café.

I nod. "Thanks."

He shrugs and slices another shrivelled lemon.

Danny's not there. It's the woman again – Pat, he said her name was. But maybe that's better. Don't want to have to ask him. He might make excuses.

"What can I get you?" Pat smiles, and I can see now why Danny likes her. She looks kind. Happy.

"Um. Actually a job." I pull my face into an apology. "I know Danny," I add. Like it's worth something.

"Oh, sorry, love. There's nothing right now. Barely enough for me and Danny. Maybe in the summer. Or if he ever gets off his backside and goes to college like he ought."

"Oh. OK." He's leaving. Or he might be.

"You're a friend of his?"

"Yeah." But am I? A friend? I don't know what I am to him. Or he to me. So I blurt out, "A friend of a friend, really. Eva. His flatmate's sister."

She nods. Like it's all clear to her. I wish it was to me. "Tell you what, leave your name and number and if anything comes up I'll give you a ring."

I scrawl my name on a piece of paper then realize I don't know the number.

"It's in the book," I say. "Trevelyan. The Cliff House."

Pat frowns for a fraction of a second. Like it doesn't add up.

"My grandmother's," I say. "She died." Like that explains everything.

"Oh. I'm sorry."

"I didn't know her," I say quickly, making it all right.

"I'll find the number, love." She nods.

"Thanks." I turn to go. Then let the words out, fast, before I chicken out: "Say hi to Danny for me."

Pat nods. "Sure." But she's distracted. Won't remember.

And I walk out onto the street again, with no job, and no idea what I'm doing.

I don't feel like going back to the hotels. For more "Sorry, loves" and empty shrugs. Instead I turn right and cross the road to the front, then down the stone steps to what passes for a beach. Muddy-looking sand, piles of seaweed tangled with plastic bottles and old baby wipes. The great British seaside.

Water whips off the sea and stings my face. Even the rain is salty here. It is cold, freezing, but this idea grips me, this need, and I reach down and pull off my cowboy boots, my striped socks, roll my jeans up my calves, and then I walk down the shelving sand into the sea.

I don't go far, just a metre or so, the water reaching below my knees, but even here I can feel it, clawing and dragging at my ankles, desperately pulling me out, claiming me. The wind rushes against my back and for a second I lose my balance and stumble, stubbing my toe against something, a rock, or rubbish. My hand plunges into the water to steady myself, drenching my sleeve.

"Shit," I shout.

But the wind takes it away. No one is listening. Can't even hear me. And I long for that flat with the solar system on the ceiling and the bare board floor and Luka singing and playing and me and Cass lying on my bed, head to toe, chewing strawberry shoelaces and singing to the radio.

He's not here. My dad. Even if he was, how would I ever find him? And Danny's going. If not now, some day soon. To college. Of course. That's why he's working in the caff. Must be. Because it's hardly a career choice. Then it will be just me, Finn and Mum. And I'm not sure that's enough any more. I want something, someone else.

Tears run down my face, taking my employ-me mascara with them. I wipe them away with a sea-soaked sleeve. Salt water surrounds me, sand crunches gritty in my teeth. I want to go home.

I turn and trudge out of the shallows. Pull on my socks and boots, the cotton clammy and damp, catching on my wet feet and bloody toes. On the way back to the house I see the charity shop Mum made us take the bags to. I don't ask for a job, know they don't pay. Instead I use my last pound and buy back a thing of hers, of my grandmother's. I buy back the locket.

And later that night, I fix the broken link with a piece of cotton, and I fasten the gossamer chain around my neck and slip the cold, hard pendant under my T-shirt, against the bones of my chest. The photo still inside. A piece of him. Of me.

Het

HET IS *nine. She is in the sea with her brother, while her mother sunbathes on the tourist-packed sand. The water laps at Het's chest. She is in further than she has been before. But she likes the cold, likes the way the water stains her red swimsuit a deep maroon, likes the way her arms goosepimple, the skin tautening, then relaxing as she thrusts them into the hot sun.*

Het has to squint to see Will stamping in the shallows, pretending his plastic net is a harpoon to stab the minnows that dart around his toes. Behind him she can see their mother in her wide hat and black bikini. Het thinks she looks like a film star. Like Marlene Dietrich. It makes her mother laugh. But her father thinks she should cover up. The sun is bad for you, he says. Makes your skin grow in tight hard moles that will eat you up from the inside. Eleanor tuts, and Het thinks he is just being mean. He's an indoors person, her mother says, explaining it away.

A man has stopped to talk to Eleanor. Not her father. This man's hair is not clipped short at the back; it curls defiantly over his collar. And his shirt isn't tucked in neatly; instead it flows loose around his linen trousers and gapes open at the neck so that Het can see a scattering of white in the hair on his chest. Her mother stands, shading her eyes with her hand. And Het watches as the man touches her on her back. A big wide palm against bare skin. Het recognizes him. It is the man from the gallery in town. In his shop are pictures of the cliffs, of beaches, of blue boats bouncing on the water.

Not a stranger then, Het thinks. A friend.

Het's mother looks out to the water at her. Het waves, then turns back to the sea, the sun behind her, rays bursting out of her skin like an angel in a picture.

But then something happens. A bad thing. The cold water shifts, pulling her forwards. Sand and the world slip from beneath her and she is swallowed by the sea. Het kicks her legs but she can't see the surface any more and instead gets dragged inside a wave. Her head is pushed out of the water for a second and she tries to breathe but instead of air, water floods into her throat, as fear floods her veins, and she is tumbled against the seabed again, rocks tearing at her legs.

Het's limbs thrash helplessly against the drag, but then she feels herself being pulled again. Only this time the hold isn't watery, it is real, a person. It is the man from the gallery. His wide palms lift her up to his chest, to the silvery glint and greying hair. He is still wearing his shirt and trousers. Het is struck by this. He is in the water in his clothes. *Why didn't he take them off?* she thinks. But she clutches tight to wet white linen anyway, lies her head on his shoulder and closes her eyes.

When she wakes up she is in bed, at home. Her legs are sore against the covers, and when she peers under the sheet she can see bandages and the black thread of a stitch.

"Daddy did it," explains her mother, handing her a glass of orange squash. "Aren't you lucky to have a daddy who is so clever?"

Het nods. She is lucky. But not because of the clever man who sewed her leg up. Because of the brave one who carried her out of the sea.

And when she looks into her mother's eyes, she can see him in there too.

BILLIE

DANNY RINGS the next day.

I don't believe Mum when she hands the phone to me. But it is him. Thank God it is him, Mum too surprised to wonder how the phone she unplugged can ring at all.

"How did you get my number?" I ask, waving at Mum to disappear, and to take Finn with her.

"Pat." He laughs, like it's obvious.

"Right." So she did look it up after all.

"So are you up for it?" he asks.

My stomach spins. I don't get it. For what? I think. For him?

"Swimming," he says into the silence.

"Oh… Yeah, sure."

"You don't sound it."

"I am. It's just… How much is it?"

"Nothing," he says.

"You can't pay for me," I protest. Don't want to be his charity case.

But he laughs. "Don't worry, I won't be. I got free passes off Mercy."

"Oh. Mercy. Right." And I should sound relieved. But I don't. I'm not. And he knows it.

"It'll be fine. You'll be fine. I'll be gentle," he jokes.

I force a laugh. Then listen to the receiver humming with static as we struggle to find words again.

"So, seven, yeah?" he says eventually. "You know where the pool is? West Road."

"I know."

"I'll leave the pass at the front desk."

"OK. Thanks." I am sure now, grateful that the call is over. "So, bye." And I hang up before I hear him answer.

Finn is in my face before I've pulled myself off the floor.

"Who was that?" he asks. "Have you got a boyfriend?"

"No. God… Mum?"

But Mum's on his side. "Who was it then?"

"His name's Danny. A friend of Eva's. He's going to teach me to swim. Remember? I told you," I accuse.

"Right," Mum nods vaguely. Then she brightens. "Maybe he could teach me, too," she says, smiling.

"Yeah, right." Because we both know this won't happen.

Once Finn fell in a pond on the common, trying to get at the turtles that grow fat there; Ninja Turtles, bought in a fad after the film then turfed out when they got too big for their tanks. Mum just stood there, like she was superglued to the ground. Luka had to go in, up to his waist in his jeans and Doc Martens. Came out looking like a swamp beast, and smelling like one. Finn was fine. But Mum wasn't. Luka said she should learn then. That it wasn't fair on us. But Mum said we would just stay away from the water instead.

I look at the kitchen clock. It's four now. That gives me three hours to get ready. And it takes me all of them.

I shave my legs. Under my arms. Then try on my red bikini, the one Cass made me get for the lido last summer. Not designed for swimming, it is tiny and tight, tied at the side with long ribbons. The top just two triangles of Lycra. I look at myself in the mirror. My skin is blue-white, translucent. I should have St Tropezed like Cass, I think. She was footballer's-wife orange all year, didn't care that the palms of her hands were giveaway orange, too, or her feet grubby where the stuff clogged on dry skin. But even that would be better than this corpse standing in front of me. It'll be fine, I tell myself. He won't see me; I'll be under the water.

But when I get there he's already in the pool, the only person there, swimming lengths, his arms pounding through the water. He is at home. This is his home. The water. And me? I stop dead at the door of the changing rooms. I feel as naked as I look. I pull my towel tight around me. Think about bolting. But it's too late. He's seen me.

"Hey." It echoes off the blue tiles, a hollow muffled sound, like an empty gym, or a hospital corridor.

I raise my hand slightly, still clutching the towel around my chest.

"Getting in?" He stands up, water cascading down his chest, through the faint traces of down, to his trunks. I look away. In case he sees me. Sees what I'm seeing.

I have to do it. I turn away and drop the towel, piling it on the bench. All the time feeling his eyes on my pale skin, on the too-small bikini. I don't look at him as I turn and slip quickly into the shallow end, clutch on to the bar. I feel myself shiver.

"You OK?" He's next to me now.

"Yeah. Just… It's cold."

"Well, we should get going then."

I nod, though every inch of me is saying no. No, I don't want to do this, can't do this, can't let you see me like this, scrabbling on the surface like a three-year-old.

But he hears it. Hears my silent dissent.

"You'll be fine," he says. "Promise. Just lie back."

And think of England. I hear Cass's words in my head and smile. Her way of getting through anything. School. Leon. The abortion.

So I do. I lie back in the water. Legs and arms out

like a starfish. I feel his hands beneath me, supporting the small of my back.

"Relax," he says. "You're tensing up."

I try. But it's hard. All I can think is that I'm here, in this strange place, with this boy I barely know, his fingers on the tie of my top.

"Shut your eyes, Billie. You're thinking too much. You need to let go."

Yeah right, I think. But I do as I'm told. Close my eyes. Tip my head back until my ears are under the water. Until I can hear the slosh and the muffled echo of the deep. The water flows over me, thick and soft. Holding me. And it is. It is holding me. I can't feel his fingers any more. He has let go. I open my eyes and jerk my head up, arms flailing. Water fills my throat and I can't breathe; I'm choking.

But he's laughing. Right in front of me, while I cough chlorine over him.

I can't speak; wave my hands at him. Stop looking at me, I think.

But he doesn't. He grasps my arms. "You did it. You floated, Billie. You floated!"

I hang my head, gasping for breath. Feel him pat me on the back. It works. I feel snot catching in my throat, cough it out. I can speak again.

I wipe it away. "Gross, huh?"

"Kind of." He laughs. "But who cares? You swam."

"No I didn't," I argue. "I just lay there."

"Next time we'll try to move," he says.

"Can't I just float?" I ask.

He laughs. "For today," he concedes, "yeah, we can just float."

And for an hour that's what we do. I float on my back, eyes open now, watching the dark sky while he floats next to me then sculls to the side, wrapping himself in a towel and watching while I lie still on the surface.

Afterwards he walks me back into town.

"So you're looking for work?"

"How did you—?"

"Same way I got your number. Pat."

I nod. Of course. Well, the secret's out now.

"You should ask Eva. Her mum works up at the Laurels. It's a care home. They always need cleaners."

I look over at him, unsure. "Won't Eva want it?"

"You must be joking. Eva wouldn't touch it with a bargepole."

"Right." Like Cass. Cass wouldn't even go to one of those places to visit her own nan. Said it smelt of pee and cabbage and death.

He writes down her address on the back of a receipt.

"So, Thursday for swimming, yeah? Same time?"

Thursday. It's only two days away. But I don't say no. I watch as he walks back towards the front, still smiling. Then open the receipt out, turn it over to read Eva's address. And something else too. A phone number. His.

Het

HET LEANS back on her arms and looks at her stomach, tan against the scarlet of her bikini. She inspects it, this stretch of skin, spreads her hands over it, feeling the heat of the last sun of the day, of the last days of summer. Then pushes gently, looking for something else. Something underneath that she knows is there but cannot see. Not yet.

"Hey." A voice calls out to her.

Het looks up and out to sea. Searches for him in the shallows. The tide is coming in; it's safe to swim now. And he is strong. Strong enough for the undertow. Though he is lean, his shoulders and arms are muscled from days of rigging at the fair.

He stands, water running down his chest, hair dripping, body sleek with it. Het searches his face for the answer. An answer he has been seeking in the water, in the rhythm of his arms rising and falling, his legs kicking steadily, the cold of the water against his flesh.

He sits down next to her. Rubs at his hair with a threadbare towel, lets it fall into his lap. "What about your dad?" he asks.

"I don't care about my dad," she replies. Her voice scarred with petulance.

"You should," he says softly. "He cares about you."

She snorts. "No he doesn't."

"Your mum then."

Het sits up, crosses her legs. "They don't matter. It's not theirs. It's ours."

Tom reaches for her hand. Grasps it, making her look at him properly.

"They won't make it easy."

She shrugs. "I've thought about it. We can go up to London, stay with Martha for a bit. You can play piano in the bars and I can work too, later. After."

"Doing what?"

"Oh, I don't know. I'll work in a café. Write a book. Something. Anything." Het pulls her hand away and wraps her arms around her knees, holding herself tight. "I've got money," she says.

"Poor little rich girl."

"Screw you," she says quietly.

She goes to stand but he pulls her back and into him.

"Sorry. I'm sorry," he whispers into her hair. "I didn't mean it. It's just… It's not a book or TV, Het. It's real."

"Don't you think I know that?" she says. "I'm not Cinderella. And there's no fairy godmother going to come and save me. There's…"

But he's shushing her now, rocking her gently.

"I'll save you," he says.

Het thinks about this. "We can save each other," she says finally.

"Deal," he says. And he moves back so he can look at her, drink her in. Then he looks down at her tummy. Puts his hand on it. "Do you think Cinderella ever got pregnant?" he says.

Het laughs. It's going to be all right. They are going to be all right.

BILLIE

EVA LIVES out on the edge of town, in one of the tight terraces. It's nearly nine when I knock on the door but I figure she's hardly one for early nights or homework. She leans against the doorframe, sizing me up, wondering what I want from her. When it's not her I want at all.

"Is your mum in?"

"No." Her voice is tinged with suspicion. "What do you want her for?"

"Work. Danny said there might be a job at the home."

"She's round Bernie's." Like I know who that is.

"Oh. OK." I turn to go. But Eva has other ideas.

"You can wait if you want. She's only gone to borrow a plunger."

I look past her down the corridor. Can see the front room flicker with TV glow. "OK. Thanks."

She walks into the light and I follow, sit on a sagging yellow chair, while she slumps on the sofa, an ashtray balanced on the arm, spilling its contents over the white vinyl. On the floor an overweight Staffie is eating what looks like a Mars bar. The room stinks. Of fags and dog and this-is-it.

Eva flicks an orange lighter, dips the tip of a Marlboro in the flame. "Where'd you see Danny then?"

"The pool," I say hesitantly, like I'm giving something away. A secret. Then I remember nothing happened. Not really. Not that you could use as evidence. Though it doesn't feel that way.

"You smell of bleach," Eva observes.

I smile, shrug. "So, you and Danny…?" I ask. Because I don't get her, where she fits in. And I'm scared of where it might be. Or where she wants it to be.

"Me and Danny nothing. He's Jake's best mate. Been around since I was born. His mum and my mum were at school together. Our school. Can you believe it? The minute I'm sixteen I am so out of this dump."

I look around and nod. Though I know it's not the room she means.

"We're close," she adds. Then looks at me slyly, gauging a reaction. "Never done it though."

"Oh," I feign indifference. But it's not enough.

"What about you?"

"What about me?" I bat it back.

"You into him?"

"I… I don't know—" But I'm saved by the sound of a key turning in the lock and the bustle of Eva's mum stamping her feet on the doormat.

"All right, Eva?" she calls.

"In here," she replies, stubbing her cigarette out in a heap of ash and fag ends. Though it's hardly a secret.

Eva's mum is the spit of her daughter, all tight curls and sly eyes. The only giveaway is the lines around her lips, creasing her mouth into a puckered hole. She looks at me, trying to work out who I am.

"This is Billie. She's after work up the home."

Eva's mum nods. "How old are you?"

"Sixteen," I say. "Seventeen in a few months."

"You at school?"

"Yes. No. Well, I will be, after Easter."

She sighs. And I worry that it's over. But she's just thinking.

"It won't be regular, like. Just when we need cover. But I could use someone Thursday. We'll see after that. Maybe you can do after school or weekends."

"Great. Yeah, anything."

"The pay's not much mind. Minimum."

"I don't care. Really."

"Fine. Well, be up there at ten. Ask for Debs."

"Debs," I repeat.

"That's me."

"Right. Thanks."

I think she's going to go then, but instead she looks hard at me, like she's trying to see inside. Like Finn used to do, when he claimed he had special powers.

"Where you from?" she says finally.

"London," I say. "But my mum grew up here." Like that makes it all right. Makes me one of them.

"Right," she says, lost for a minute. Then, "So, Thursday at ten."

"I'll be there." I smile. "Thanks, Debs."

She nods and walks out, heading towards the kitchen with her plunger and twenty Bensons and the dog trailing behind her.

"Thanks, Debs," Eva repeats all sing-song, like it's a joke.

"I'd better go," I say.

Eva shrugs. "Whatever."

I laugh. "See you around."

"Yeah." She pauses, narrows her eyes. "I'll probably be at Jake and Danny's at the weekend. If you're about."

"Great, yeah." And I cringe as I hear myself. An eager puppy. Desperate for affection. "Whatever," I add quickly.

"Whatever," she repeats.

Eva closes the door behind me. I stand in the street, smell the smoke on my skin, in my hair. I shake it, letting rain spatter onto my face. Do your worst, I think. Because it doesn't matter. Nothing matters.

I've got a job. An honest-to-God minimum-wage job.

And I can swim. Well, float.

And it's all because of Danny. And as I think his name
I feel the butterflies dance, but not in fear, in delight.

Het

HET HAS seen the girl before. Seen her with her friends at the fair, slinking round Tom and Jimmy. Smiles sticky with Twilight Teaser and legs shiny with Hawaiian Tropic Factor 2. Kelly something, her name is.

She is beautiful, Het thinks. In a way. Obvious, her mother would say. All that flesh. Her breasts pushed up in a Wonderbra, skirt barely below her knickers. Will and Jonty call her a townie, a slapper. But she knows Will's had his hands inside that black lace, whatever he says to their parents. Jonty says he's got better taste. Lets his eyes fall on Het's chest, move down to her crotch. She shudders.

Kelly is walking towards her now. The others a step behind, like bridesmaids, or henchmen. They stop dead in front of her in a cloud of Impulse and cigarettes.

"You're Het, aren't you?"

Het nods, knowing that being Het is a bad thing right now.

Kelly considers this, blows out a careful ring of smoke, tips her head to one side. "Stay away from him. He don't belong to you."

Het knows she means Tom. "He doesn't belong to anybody," she replies.

One of the girls laughs, but Kelly jabs her elbow into her. "What's that supposed to mean?"

"Just that." Het shrugs. "He can make his own mind up."

Kelly snorts. Then tries a different tack. "He only wants you for one thing, you know?"

"Maybe," Het concedes. But she knows it's a lie. It's not that. It's more; it's everything. And they know it too.

The laughing girl tugs at Kelly's crop top. Kelly takes a step back, links arms with her.

"You're right — she's not worth it," she sneers. And they turn in sync like Rockettes and walk back down the street, cheap heels click-clacking in unison on the gum-sticky pavement.

Het sees the laughing girl's name across the back of her top, spelled out in glittery gold iron-on patches. It says DEBS.

BILLIE

THE LAURELS sounds like this lush green oasis, but it's anything but. A hulking great lump of granite on the main road, no one else would live here, no one who had a choice anyway. There are no trees to speak of and the rain hits it from every angle. As I walk up the gravel-bare drive, I hear the rumble of lorries on the A30. Sweet dreams.

Inside it's like they've tried to recreate some *Care Homes from Hell* cliché. From wipe-clean furniture screwed to the floor to the windows that never open. And the heat. I swear it's a hundred degrees inside. I touch my finger to a radiator and feel my skin burn. The place is like a Lock-and-Lock box, keeping in the prickling smell of ammonia and hopelessness. The TV room gives a nod to comfort: fitted carpet and covered chairs. But they're old, and the smell is worse here, the fabric has absorbed the farts and sweat and stale breath of generations. It sticks to everything. To them. And to me.

"You don't need to talk to them," Debs tells me. "You're not paid to do that."

And at first I'm relieved because I don't know what to say. But when I see them staring at *This Morning*, not really listening, just watching the pictures moving, I want to talk. I want to shout.

Where are their families? I think. Have they just left them here? Forgotten about them? And I wonder what will happen to Mum when she's like this. What I'll do when she's too old to look after herself, let alone me, and it's my and Finn's turn to look after her instead. "Take me to Switzerland," she used to joke, "before I think I'm the Queen of Sheba." But sometimes she already does. And anyway, I don't know if she'll get that far. Always thought there might be a chance she'd go in her own way, in her own time.

Mum said I didn't need to do this.

I'm sitting at the breakfast table bolting down cake and cranberry juice, because that's all there is, and she's telling me she's got a plan. That she's going to turn Cliff House into a B&B. Do it all up in off-white with driftwood mirrors and proper sheets, the kind that come with a thread count.

So I lie and say I need money for art stuff. That I'm saving up, for myself. Mum says it won't be easy. That it won't be like rinsing out the bath here. It will be proper work. Hard work. I laugh. Say it will be fine. I'll be fine.

But it's not. I'm not. The doors swing open, bringing a hot gush of stale air from the kitchen. Stench of meat and potatoes and root vegetables boiled too long. Of schools and old people. Of Nonna and Nonno. Mum's parents were lucky, I think. Lucky this isn't where they ended up. Lucky to be gone. And then I start. Want to pinch myself, throw cold water on me. Because that's an awful thing to say. Even think. A Cass thing. An Eva thing.

"Oi, Billie."

I turn and see Debs waiting for me, one Marigold hand on her hip, a bucket in the other.

"Bedrooms. I'll show you which are yours."

I shake myself. Like it will clear my head. But all it does is waft another gust of hot stewy air around me. So I say goodbye to a wall of silence, and follow Debs up the clacky tacky lino stairs.

"You do the odds," she says.

At first I think she means oddballs, like the weirdos or something. And I think, That's not fair; it's my first day. Scared I'm going to get some Jack Nicholson nutter or a Miss Havisham in her wedding dress, wondering where her groom has gone for fifty years. But it's just the numbers. One and Three and Five all the way to Thirteen. Lucky for some.

"Hoover, dust, clean the sink and toilet, make the bed. Unless they're in it, or have peed in it," she adds.

I laugh. But it's not a joke. None of it is.

In Five a woman – I'm guessing ninety though I've never seen anyone that old, so who knows, she could have been a hundred – is lying on mauve polyester. Her skin like paper, hanging loosely over protruding bones so thin I can see her veins tracing a blue map beneath. She is a living skeleton, watching me through milky cataract eyes. I lift a mug on her bedside table to dust underneath. SUPERNAN it says. But when I put it down again Supernan starts to wail. I panic, back off, thinking I've spilt something, hurt her somehow. Because it's the sound of pain, of wounding. But Debs just comes in and tuts, and slides the mug a centimetre to the left. The wailing stops instantly.

"Fussy old so-and-so," she says, rolling her eyes. "You'll get used to it." And she goes out again, back to the evens.

I finish dusting, not touching anything else, scared that if I nudge an ornament, a photograph, even slightly I'll set her off, cause her this pain that is so real it makes her scream. Supernan. I wonder who gave her that mug. Where they are now. If they know that this is what she has become.

When I go into the next room I hold my breath, praying that the sheets are dry, the bed empty, its occupant watching TV downstairs. And it is. And made, too, the duvet pulled back into place. I poke my head round the door again, check the number, in case I've got it wrong, in case Debs has already been in. But it's Seven, one of mine. Then I see him. Sitting in a chair next to the window, staring out at the patch of overgrown, rabbit-holed turf they call the garden, and the petrol station beyond it.

"Hello," I say. Just to let him know I'm here. In case I turn the Hoover on and give him a shock, or worse. Debs said it can happen. Has happened.

He turns and I can see he's not that old. Seventy or so. Younger maybe; his hair longer than the others; less military, curling over his black shirt collar in salt and pepper tendrils. His trousers are black too. Loose. He doesn't fit in here, I think. He's not old. He's not one of them. But then he speaks to me, and I click.

"You took your time."

"I... I'm sorry, I'm new."

"New?" he says. Not getting it. "Where's your mother? I want to see your mother."

Christ. He thinks I'm his granddaughter. I don't know whether to play along or run and hide. In the end I try the truth.

"I'm Billie," I say. "The cleaner."

He stares at me blankly. His eyes still dark, not the faded milky blue of Supernan. He can see clearly. But somewhere the picture of me is getting sidetracked, misdirected, and re-emerging from his memory, mixed with another girl, another time.

Then, *click*, he's here.

"Cleaner." He nods, like this makes sense now. "Bloody awful job. But someone's got to do it. I had a job, you know. All mine it was. It's gone now. It all goes."

"Right," I say. Like I understand. Maybe I do. A bit. That in the end, all there is is us, and what's inside our heads. The rest is ephemera.

He lifts up his legs so I can hoover under the chair, laughing like a child as he does it. But when I flick the switch off and reel in the cord, he's gone again. Inside. Gone back to staring out at the garage and the gloom.

Later I tell Debs about him. About his granddaughter.

She snorts. "He hasn't even got one," she says. "Never married. No kids, no grandkids. Some old girlfriend paid for him to come here, they say. Then left him money in her will. Or he'd be down the council home by now."

My heart sinks to think there's a place worse than this. Worse than the cheap seats and the bleakness and the promise of death that hangs over everything, clutching at the curtains, the carpet, like another stale smell.

"Poor old bugger," Debs adds. "He don't even know who he is most of the time."

But I'm not sure. There was a second there when he knew. When he recognized it all. But it was only a second. And that's not enough, not for anyone.

ELEANOR

ELEANOR HAS seen him once before. Standing on the front, eyes closed, letting the heat of a June midday beat down on his face and chest. Roger pulled her quickly past him, muttering under his breath, but she looked back, fascinated by this sun-worshipper in his paint-spattered fisherman's smock and jeans. Roger never wore jeans. They were working men's clothes. Beatnik clothes. He wore suits, or scrubs, his only concession to a Saturday to remove his tie. But this man; this man doesn't care what people think. What he looks like. Eleanor envies him.

When she sees him again, she is sitting in the window of the Grand, drinking Earl Grey and ersatz coffee with Carol Lister. He walks past, a cap on his head, something rolled up under his arm.

"Who is that?" Eleanor asks.

Carol looks up, her lips as thin as her waspish waist, as her humour. Eleanor loathes her. Thinks that beneath the veneer of Yves Saint Laurent and Rive Gauche she is cheap, vulgar. But her husband is a colleague of Roger's. And she does have her uses. An unwavering interest in everyone else's affairs being one of them.

"That," she intones with the surety of knowledge, "is Alexander Shaw. Bought the Blue Gallery three months ago. Used to live in London. Chelsea apparently. Very chi-chi." She raises her eyebrows at this. Like Chelsea is something to be despised, pitied. Though Eleanor guesses Carol would leave Seaton and the Grand in a New York minute for a seat at anywhere on the King's Road.

"Married?" Eleanor asks, affecting disinterest, as if it would be impossible for him to be because he's so odd. Because Carol would swoop at the first hint of— What? A crush? Not that Eleanor means it that way, she says to herself. She is a married woman. It's just, he seems so different. So elsewhere.

"Not," replies Carol, picking an invisible hair from a macaroon. "Good God, what is this place?" To no one. Then back to Eleanor. "Those artistic types often don't."

She spits out artistic in the same inverted commas in which she encased Chelsea. Like it's pretentious. Or pretend. Made-up. But he's not made-up. He's real. More real than the man she shares a bed with every night. Who pretends that they are happy, pretends he loves her, as she pretends to love him.

Or maybe she does. She married him, didn't she? But it all seemed so inevitable. The dates, the dance, the ring, the reception at the golf club. It will be babies next. Because that's what you do. People like Carol. And her. But when she sees Alexander Shaw, she wants to step out of her life, wants to stand with the sun on her face and her head back. Wants freedom.

The next day she walks past the gallery. Every day for a week she stops at the window, pretending to be absorbed by the watercolours and seascapes. "Daubings" Roger calls them. "Amateur. Not worth a penny."

But Eleanor likes them.

Then, one afternoon, she forgets to try, and lets herself become transfixed by the turquoise of a seascape. She doesn't see him get up, walk across the bleached boards, open the door.

"Hello."

She yelps, her reverie shaken.

"Sorry," he says. "I didn't mean…"

"No. I was just… Who's the artist?"

"Do you like them?"

She nods.

"In that case, I don't mind telling you. It's me."

Her eyes flick to the lower-left corner. There it is: A. Shaw, in tiny italics. God, how stupid. "I… I didn't realize. It's … beautiful."

"There's more inside."

She shakes her head quickly. "I have to go," she says.

"Another time, then."

"Yes. Another time."

And there will be. And another. And another.

BILLIE

I FINISH at four. Six hours of scrubbing, wiping, vac-
uuming, dusting. Of stacking dishwashers with gravy-
smeared plates and unloading them again, ignoring the
brown caked-on grease that has hardened to an immovable
crust. Of eating my lunch in a tiny office, leaning against
a filing cabinet, trying not to listen to Debs on her mobile,
laughing and swearing and slagging off some woman in
Room Four, who peed the bed again.

Six hours. By the time I step out into the damp sea-heavy
air, every inch of me is crawling with the feel of nylon,
every inch smells of old people.

I want to wash, to shower it off me. But when I get

home the bathroom door is locked and I can hear the buzz of the portable radio playing something classical. Mum is in the bath, has been for an hour, Finn says. So I make us toast and watch a game show. Play along as Finn tries to guess which box has the fortune in it.

"What are you doing here anyway?" Finn speaks and a mouthful of buttery crumbs fly out onto the green velvet of the armchairs. "I thought you were going swimming."

"Oh my God. Swimming." I had forgotten. How? I stand, trying to remember where I've left my towel. The bikini.

"Can't you take me?" Finn pleads. "I can swim."

"No. I know. But … it's a lesson. I can't look after you too." Don't want to tell him that I want Danny to myself. That I don't want my kid brother tagging along.

"I don't need looking after."

I laugh. "Listen. Tell her … tell her I'll be back late."

"Whatever." He bites off another mouthful. "You smell."

I plunge my head under the water, one hand holding my nose, Danny gripping the other. Chlorine rushes into my ears so that I am locked in this underwater world, bleach washing away the stew and polish. Then I stand up, burst through the surface to take a heaving lungful of air. I am clean.

This time, when I lie back and he lets go, I don't panic and swallow dead-skin water, I don't rush to find my feet. I let the water hold me.

"Kick your legs," he says.

And I do. And then I'm moving backwards, the water rushing past my ears. And I know it's dumb, but I feel like I'm flying. And I know now how Finn feels, why he screams and hoots when he's in the water. Because it's incredible. How can Mum be scared of this? I think. How can she not want to feel like this?

He gets chips afterwards, and we sit on the front.

"Go on," he says.

I realize I'm starving, with the thrill of it, the effort. And the two days of cake and canapés. I suck the vinegar off the hot crisp potato and smile. It's the taste of the sea. Of Seaton. Of this new life.

"Come back to the flat," he says.

And it's not a question. So there's only one answer.

"OK."

Jake and Mercy are there. And Eva. She's lying full out on the sofa, eyes shut, nodding in time to the throb of some CD. When she opens them, I see her pupils are wide, black. Smell the air above her, above them all, sickly sweet with weed. She waits to see my reaction. But I don't flinch. Don't take the spliff either though. Cass used to smoke; Luka too. I tried it, a couple of times – another secret – but I didn't like the taste or the dizziness or the glassy eyes looking at you but seeing someone else. No one finishing a sentence. It scared me. Reminded me of Mum on her bad days. Why would I want to be like that? So I let the scorn shine in Eva's eyes and the smoke and conversation drift over me. And it's only when the silence ticks on for more than the time it takes to have a toke that I realize they're waiting for me to answer.

"Sorry, what?" I'm sitting on the floor, next to Danny, my back against a bookcase, my shoulder a breath from his.

"How come your mum left and then came back?"

"I don't know," I say. And it's the truth.

"You going to stay?" Eva is watching me, waiting.

"I don't know. I think so. I hope so." And I do. At that moment, I really do. But then Eva has to ask.

"What about your dad?" She takes a long pull on the spliff. Holds it in. Then breathes out the words in a cloud of smoke. "Not Luka. The real one. Where is he?"

Suddenly the insects jerk awake in my stomach. "I don't know," I say, defensively. My fingers are shaking. I push my hands under my thighs.

"Did he leave?" she pokes again, digging at the wound like a dog at a bone.

I could tell her, I think. Tell them all why I'm really here. Ask them if they know him. If they've ever heard of a man called Tom. But as I hear the absurdity of the words ringing out in my head I know I won't speak them aloud.

"I never met him," I say.

"What's his name?"

"Tom, OK?" I blurt. "What about yours, where's he?"

Eva's pupils narrow to a pinprick, so that she looks

alien. And I think, I've done it now. I've messed up. That he's dead. Or in prison.

But then Jake laughs. "He's down the Red Lion, same as every night."

And Eva smiles, like I've passed some test. Bored now, she turns to her brother. "Do you remember when he…"

But I don't hear the end. I feel Danny's hand slide under mine, his fingers reach and curl around my own. I check Eva, in case she's seen, but she's still talking. Off on one about some other night, some other year. He squeezes gently, then pulls away again. And my heart slows, the wings stop beating.

"Why don't you ask your mum?" he says quietly. "About him, I mean?"

"I… It's too complicated," I say eventually.

Way too complicated. When I was a kid, tiny, she told me he was a famous sailor, Tom the Magnificent. That he was busy fighting sea monsters and pirates, protecting mermaids. That he would only come back when there were no more battles to be fought. And I would make her tell me stories of the giant squid and the whales, of how I was lucky he was out there, keeping the seas safe. Again and again I would beg. Until I was old enough to know that *Moby-Dick* was just a story, and pirates, the ones with eye patches and parrots, died a long time ago.

Then she would tell me she waited for him, but he never came. That he wasn't a brave hero. He was a coward.

Tom the Feeble. Tom the Weak. And we didn't need one of those. That was the last time I asked. I was nine.

Cass said we could hunt him down anyway, as soon as I was sixteen. We could go to some place up in town and demand my birth certificate and stuff. But on my sixteenth she was too busy chasing Ash. And I'd already seen my birth certificate by then anyway, found it stuffed in a drawer full of bills. Under FATHER it just said, "Unknown".

And I've been here long enough now to know that I'm never going to bump into him. That it's as likely as him fighting a serpent or kissing a mermaid. That I'll never get to ask all those questions I've written in my head:

Does he like liquorice too?

Does he eat the biscuit off the top of an Oreo then scrape off the white inside with his teeth?

Did he love her?

Did he know about me?

Is that why he left?

Eva is asleep on the sofa and not even Jake can make her move. Danny walks me home.

He doesn't touch my hand again. But the moment hangs there between us, lit up.

"What about yours?" I say.

"My what?"

"Family."

"Not much to tell. My mum and sister have moved away, gone up-country to live with my stepdad."

Stepdad. I didn't know. But why would I? I never asked.

He can see me working it out. Like a puzzle. "He's a copper," he adds. Like that explains it.

"Why didn't you go with them?" I can't imagine letting Mum go without me.

He shrugs. "I don't know. Felt like I was intruding, I guess. She's his, you know? My sister. Half-sister," he corrects himself. "They're all right though. I see them at Christmas and stuff."

Then I ask him the million dollar question. "What about your dad. Your actual one."

"Up-country, too. Comes back in season. When the work's good."

"What's he like?"

"I dunno. Looks a bit like me. That's it."

"Don't you want to know more?"

"I know enough."

I think he's cross with me. But it's not that. It's genuine. He doesn't need him. He's like Mum. And I wonder who his family is now.

We stop at the gate. I lift the latch up, hear the metal clunk and whine as it moves on its rusting hinges.

"You want to swim again?" he says quickly.

I stop and bring my eyes up to meet his.

"Tomorrow?" Shit. It's so obvious. I'm obvious.

"I can't. The café," he says. "We stay open late on Fridays and Saturdays."

"Right. Sure. Whatever." I try to affect nonchalance. But I'm pretty sure it comes off as nerves.

"Sunday. In the morning?"

"I have to work," I say. Glad of the excuse.

"Monday then?"

"What time?"

"Not sure. I'll call. Let you know."

"OK. Monday. It's a date." Oh God. I feel blood rush to my cheeks, so hot I'm sure the air around me must steam. "I didn't mean—"

But he doesn't skip a beat. "A date," he says. "See you." And I watch him walking backwards, watching me. Then he sticks his hands in his pockets and turns. I realize my fingers are gripping the cold iron of the gate latch. The knuckles white. I release them. A date. Is it? Do I want it to be?

And I know I do.

ELEANOR

AT FIRST Eleanor uses the picture as an excuse to see him. She goes back two, three times, stands and admires the fine brush strokes around the shoreline, the way the light catches the surface of the water, waiting for him to beckon her in.

She finds him fascinating; his otherness. The way he smiles so easily. The way he smells – of oil and turpentine. She will learn to love that smell.

On her fourth visit she realizes she has fallen in love. A ridiculous, inconvenient, overwhelming love. But she cannot tell him. And cannot have him. So instead she transfers this feeling into the blues and greens of the water-colour. She becomes obsessed with it, and wants it, wants it badly. But it is two hundred pounds. And that sort of money *he will trace, will see the missing cheque stub, watch its passage out of the account, as he runs through her spending, line after line.*

"You could work for it," Alex says one day.

"Wh–what?" she stammers.

"No... I don't mean— It's just ... I could do with someone to help. Just the odd morning. So I can paint. It's a waste of light, sitting in here."

She knows what Roger will say if she asks him, asks for permission. So she blurts out a "yes". So it's too late. So he cannot change her mind for her. So by the time she sits down to supper, she is already planning what she will wear.

Roger eyes her over the rim of his whiskey tumbler. "What in God's name do you want a job for?"

"It will be good for me," she explains. "Get me out of the house."

"What will the Listers think?"

Eleanor pictures Carol, her wasp-thin waist and wasp-sharp comments. She knows exactly what she will think. But it wasn't a question. He doesn't need an answer.

"It will have to stop soon," he says. "Once you're pregnant, you'll have no time for a job."

"I know," she says.

He nods. And, satisfied he has won a small victory, he goes back to his soup, the conversation over.

But Eleanor's head is still full of words. It will come to an

end, she thinks. All good things come to an end. But for now,
it is just the beginning.

He gives her the painting the first week.

  She protests. "I haven't earned it yet."

  But he pushes it on to her. "A gift, then. You can say it's
worthless. That way he won't guess."

  "Guess what?" she says. But the minute the words leave
her lips, she already knows the answer.

She doesn't hang the painting. She wraps it in a blanket
and hides it in the attic, leaning against a box of her school
certificates, her gymnastic awards. Her old life. She doesn't
need them any more, just as she doesn't need the painting.
Because now she has something better. She has him.

BILLIE

SUNDAY AT the Laurels is no different to Thursday. No weekend excitement here. The same food, the same TV, the same endless waiting for death's release.

But Number Seven is different. This time he doesn't think I'm his granddaughter. Doesn't slip behind his eyes, vacant, lost. This time he nods a hello, then goes back to his book, absorbed despite the hum of the Hoover, despite my gangly frame edging around him, dusting the photographs, the stacked books. I glance at the cover of one. It is a glossy, coffee-table thing, an art book. Rothko's *Light Red Over Black*.

I saw the real thing once. At the Tate Modern. Mum took us, me and Finn, Cass tagging along for something to do while her mum got her nails done. We were eleven. Cass pushed Finn in his buggy, let go of him in the Turbine Hall, Finn shrieking with delight as he careered along the concrete, hands waving at the ceiling, reaching for the light. He crashed into a woman and that was the last time Cass was put in charge of the pushchair. She got bored after that. Wanted to go to the Aquarium to see the sharks. But Mum wanted to see the Rothko, so we trailed upstairs, Cass complaining about how boring pictures were, me joining in to keep face. But when I got into the room, found myself dwarfed by these giant-tall canvases of magentas and blacks and oranges, the moaning and tutting and begging stopped. I was lost for words.

I click off the Hoover and it whirrs into a silence as heavy as the buzz before.

"I love Rothko," I say.

"Huh?" he looks up, confusion etched on his face.

I'm worried he's gone again. "Rothko." I point at the book, desperation staining my voice.

But his eyes focus, and the corners of his mouth flicker upwards into a smile. "An abstract fan, then," he observes. Not a question. But I answer anyway.

"I guess. Not Pollock though. Or Hodgkin."

"You know your art."

I shrug. But he's interested; lit up suddenly.

"What's your name?"

"Billie. Billie Paradise."

"Funny surname."

"It should be Trevelyan," I explain. "But my mum changed it."

"Trevelyan," he rolls the word around his tongue. Like he's testing it. "I once knew a Trevelyan. Worked for me."

"Will?" I blurt out. But I know before it leaves my lips that it couldn't have been. He was, what, eighteen when he died? Too young for a job, surely. And, anyway, he was at boarding school most of the time.

"No. A girl. Woman. What was her name?"

"I…" I want to say Het – Mum. But it couldn't have been her, either. She never worked when she was growing up. She told me. Her father forbade it.

"What was it?" he asks someone. Me? No – himself. His eyes narrow in anger as he searches for a memory, a secret that has been locked up in his head.

"It doesn't matter," I say.

"But it does. It does… God damn it." He claps the book covers shut, sending motes of dust flying about in a shaft of light.

It's then I notice.

"Look," I say. "The sun." I sound like a child. Or like I'm talking to one.

But it is a new, child-like thing of wonder. Because after weeks of relentless rain, the room is suddenly bathed in gold. Shiny. Outside it glints off the windscreens of the cars waiting for petrol.

"It's hot," he says. "Too hot."

I turn and look at him sitting there, swaddled in a

thick, cable-knit fisherman's jumper. The double-glazing like a magnifying glass, focusing the sun on the wool, while behind him the radiator chugs out its own infernal heat.

"I'll open the window," I say. But when I try to lift the handle I realize it's locked, and there's no key here. In case he tries to jump, I realize. To escape.

When I look back to apologize I can see him struggling. Twisting his arms this way and that, like he's Houdini in a straitjacket. Only I can tell there's no *ta-da* moment with this.

"Here, let me help you."

He holds his arms out so I can pull the sleeves down and off him, free him. I take the hem in my hands, start pulling it up and over his head. But for a second, his face is covered, wrapped in grey wool, trapped in the dark. And he panics. The noise isn't human. It's a desperate, animal sound. A howl or a moo or something.

I yank the jumper down.

"It's OK," I say, trying to calm him. "I'm here. You're here."

He is dazed and confused.

"What were you doing?" he shouts.

"You were hot," I explain. "You wanted to take your jumper off. I … I was helping."

"Who are you?"

I sigh inside. But force it out. "Billie," I say. "I'm Billie. Billie Paradise."

He thinks for a minute.

"Funny surname."

"Yeah, I…" And I'm about to go into it again. The

Trevelyan thing. When I think of something else.

"What's yours?"

"What's what?"

"Sorry. Your name?"

He pauses for a moment. And I feel the desperation rise again, the butterflies. But then he turns to me. Clear. Focused.

"Shaw," he says. "Alexander Shaw."

When I get out the sun is still hanging around. And someone else with it. Mum. She's sitting on the wall at the end of the drive while Finn kicks the last kernels of pea gravel into an imaginary United goalpost, falls to his knees to the roar of an unseen crowd.

"Finn. Your knees, baby."

Mum is wearing a summer dress, her arms bare, the flesh pale and stippled with goosebumps. I flick a glance back and see Debs at the window. See the curiosity in her eyes. Or contempt, maybe. Thinking Mum's the one that needs shutting up in a home. Walking round dressed like that. I feel embarrassment flush my cheeks. For a second I hate her, Mum. Then hate myself more for caring. Why does she do this stuff?

I turn back. "What's going on?" I ask.

"Nice to see you, too." She jumps down from the wall, lands with a *thwack* on the ground. And I see what she's got on her feet. Flip-flops. Christ.

"I didn't mean... It's just that—"

"Joking, babe. Summer's here. Thought we could go to the beach."

It's March. It's freezing. But something tells me I need to shut up now, play along. So I smile, say, "Great", and try not to let her see me wrap my scarf tighter round my neck.

But as we walk back down towards the town, Mum's enthusiasm infects me.

"Look," she says. "A whole new world."

And she is right. It is a whole new world. The sunlight shimmers on the water, ricochets off slate roofs. The town is transformed, the way London is when the snow falls and muffles the dirt and noise in a blanket of clean white.

Mum links her arm through mine, Finn racing ahead. And I ignore the eyes on us. Ignore the stares and the "What the hell?"s. And instead I wrap myself in my family, like a force field, protection against the enemy. And I soak up the sun.

Mum's good mood lasts until six. She takes us digging for sandworms, then for ice cream from the Fudge Factory, the woman behind the counter laughing, saying it's the first sale she's had in months. Takes us all the way back up the hill with promises of pizza for tea and staying up late. But then we open the door, see the answerphone blinking its red eye at us. As if to say, "I know something you don't know." And everything turns to black.

There are two messages. The first is Danny. About swimming. I'm to meet him at two because he's on an early and the pool will be empty then. And so my stomach is already alive by the time the second message kicks in. Mum's hanging round me, Finn under her arm singing "Billie and Danny up a tree, K. I. S. S. I. N. G."

"Ssshh," I say. "I can't hear." Thinking maybe Cass has finally got round to ringing. Or it's work. Or Danny again. Changing the time. Cancelling. Letting me off, and my butterflies out.

But it's a man's voice. Deeper than Danny. Older. His voice rich with breeding, money. A sugar-daddy voice, Cass would say. And this sugar daddy has a name.

"Henrietta… Het… It's Jonty."

He pauses, wondering what to say next, I guess. Leaving a gap big enough for Finn to fit in, "Who's Jonty?"

The name jolts my memory. I can see it spelled out in Eleanor's looped italics underneath a photo of two boys with a carrot-nosed snowman. *Will and Jonty, Christmas 1977.* It's someone from back then. Someone Mum knew.

I turn to her, looking for the same recognition. But whoever he is, whatever he is to her, she doesn't want to remember, and, instead of nostalgia, anger floods her eyes.

I reach for the answerphone, trying to cover it before she can hit DELETE. Instead she pushes it to the floor and tries to stamp on it with her pink Havaianas. All the time she's swearing to herself, at me, at him.

"For Christ's sake, Billie. This is why I told you to turn it off."

"Who is he?"

"Nobody. God."

Then I realize. Or I think I do. It makes sense. It's so obvious. "He's my dad," I blurt out.

Mum looks up at me, her face pale, her cheeks flushed with effort, or embarrassment. And I think, This is it; she's going to tell me.

But instead she shakes her head. "No, Billie, he's not. He's nobody. A nobody." And then she raises her leg and brings it hard down on the answerphone again. "Nobody," she repeats. "Nobody."

"Mum, stop," Finn pleads.

But she doesn't. She stamps on and on. Which would be funny if it wasn't so tragic. And then, finally, I hear a crack. And Mum stops and steadies herself against the wall, her breath coming fast and hard.

Finn is crying. But Mum can't hear him. All she can hear is the voice inside her head. And the voice tells her to walk away. To shut herself off. And she does. So it's me who crouches on the hallway floor, holds Finn, hauls him up and then lies him down on the sofa, scans through the channels to find cartoons, makes him pizza for tea.

And that's how we sit for three hours. Our faces sticky with cheese, our eyes glazed with *Transformers*. Just me and Finn. At nine, Mum still hasn't come down, so it's me who tells him he has to go to bed, makes him clean his teeth, reads him four pages of Harry Potter before I realize his eyes are shut and he is lost in another world, fighting his own dragons. And demons.

Mum's door is still closed. And I should go to bed. But I'm too wired. I know I won't sleep. Not like this. So instead I get my paper and pencils, and I draw.

I draw Finn and Luka. Draw Mum, in her sundress, in her own March summer. I draw Danny. His soft smile, his lean chest, his long fingers. I draw until my blood stops singing, till my eyes ache and my hands are stiff. Then I let sleep take me away too.

HET

HET LOATHES Christmas. The enforced jollity. The baubles and tinsel and wrapping paper, promising the earth but delivering disappointment in the shape of another hat and scarf and thin, insipid gravy.

But worse is Boxing Day. Every year her parents insist on having half of Seaton around for cocktails. Or rather, her father does. Het can see the weariness in her mother's red-rimmed eyes; weariness she chases away with Optrex and sherry.

This year Het is dressed in some absurd taffeta thing her mother has bought from Dingles in Plymouth. The boned emerald silk squashes Het's breasts and digs into her back, leaving weals on the faded tan of her skin. She can feel the lace underskirt rubbing against her bare legs. At least she won *the battle of the American Tan tights.*

"You look a delight, dear." Carol Lister kisses her on both cheeks while blowing out a thin seam of Pall Mall smoke.

I look like a Christmas Fairy, thinks Het. But she doesn't say so. She smiles thinly and murmurs her thanks.

Carol arches an overplucked eyebrow, giving her the strange air of an emaciated drag queen. "Jonty's here, you know," she whispers conspiratorially.

"Oh," says Het. "Well, I'll be sure to look out for him."

"You do that." Carol draws slowly on her cigarette.

But Het forgets to. Instead he finds her.

Het takes a Twiglet from a crystal bowl on the dining table and sucks off the salty coating and with it a memory of Christmases past. She wishes she were seven not seventeen. Wishes she were small enough to see the world through a sea of pantyhosed and navy-serged legs, small enough to drink sugary Ribena instead of the sour claret her father has pushed into her hand, small enough to slip under the table still. Away from the smoke and the sound and the silent hating, hidden by a curtain of white linen in her own small world.

But is she so big? She doesn't feel it. Feels like she's playing dress-up. Her feet sliding around in her mother's court shoes, a dress she would never have chosen, will never wear again. She looks around. No one is watching. The doctors and dentists, the great and the good of the county, are absorbed in themselves and soused in festive spirit. So, quickly, quietly,

Het drops the Twiglet on the floor, crouches as if to retrieve it, then slides neatly along the carpet to the safety of the table.

She sits cross-legged on the sage green, the white table-cloth trailing around her, cocooning her. Too tall now to lie on her tummy, her ear against the floor, listening to the thud of footsteps and hum of conversation. Instead she hears the clunk of glasses above her. The pop of a champagne cork and the ripple of a cheer at the extravagance of it, the indulgence. Hears the murmur of small talk, of golf and gardening. Then a change in tone, and her father's restrained anger, his "Why is that man Shaw here?" Her mother's gritted-teeth reply, that it would look worse if he had not been invited.

She hears all of it, from the safety of her hiding place. Smells it too. A distant haze of Nina Ricci and sweat and cigars. And something else. Aftershave and money. But close, overpoweringly close. It is the smell of an intruder.

"Still playing hide-and-seek, Hetty?"

She feels her stomach leap. "Jonty."

She doesn't look at him. His breath is hot and whiskey-sour on her neck. His lips so close she can feel the vibration against her when he speaks.

"God, you're gorgeous."

Then his lips are on her neck, his tongue warm and wet, leaving slug-trails of saliva on her skin. Like a Labrador, Het thinks. She pushes him off.

"Stop it."

"What's the matter? Scared Daddy might see? He'd be over the bloody moon if he knew it was me."

"No. It's… I just… I don't want to."

"Frigid little cow," he hisses.

Maybe I am, Het thinks. Maybe that's why she feels like this. Empty. Dead.

It's not the first time he's kissed her. That was aged thirteen, in a game of sardines that she had begged to be excused from. But Eleanor insisted and so Jonty squeezed into her mother's wardrobe, amongst the silk and the jacquard and the fox-fur coats. Het made a wish that this were Narnia and she could disappear into the snow behind and run away. But there was no lion, no witch, just hard oak against her spine.

"Want to play blue murder?" he whispered in the dark.

"What's that?" she asked.

"This," he said. And then she felt him. His fat lips on her mouth. His body pressing against hers.

But Het felt nothing. Not then. Not when he pulled her behind a bush during a game of French cricket. Or in the cinema, when he pushed his hand up her skirt, his fingers gripping her bare thigh, possessing her, trapping her in a place where she couldn't scream.

Each time Het lets him. Hoping this will be the moment the earth moves, that life lives up to its Judy Blume promise.

But it never does.

"Come on," he says. "Old times' sake."

"Not here."

"Upstairs then."

And she lets him. Lets him lead her up to her bedroom. Lets him kiss her.

Not because she wants him. But because she wants to feel something, anything.

But ten minutes later, when he's bored of her unresponsive arms, when he's back downstairs braying with Will and her father about some rugby match, when she's lying on her bed, wiping the wet from her neck, she still feels nothing. And she wonders then if she ever will.

BILLIE

"TAKE FINN with you."

Mum slams a cup of coffee down on the counter, its contents slopping over the Formica and dripping a steady brown trickle onto the floor.

"What?" I say. I'm standing at the door, swimming kit in my hand. I'm late already and now she lays this on me.

She's been like it all morning. Finn set her off. Asking for Luka. Asking when his daddy was coming. And she starts banging around in the kitchen, looking for something, some plate that she has to have and none of the others will do. Then she decides she wants butterscotch Angel Delight for lunch and sends Finn down to the corner shop, shouting at me when he comes back with crisps and a packet of Chewits instead. Like it's my fault.

She's letting it buzz round her like an angry bee. That phone call. Luka. She can't think straight. The banging, the busy stuff is to block it out. I know that now. But it doesn't work.

"You heard me. Take Finn swimming."

"Yes." Finn punches the air.

And part of me wants to say yes. Because of the way she is. The way she might be going. But then I think of Danny. Of his hand on mine. And I can't. I just can't.

"No," I say.

"Why? What are you planning on doing?" Mum brushes a pool of coffee onto the floor with her hand.

"Nothing," I say quickly.

"Then take him. I want some peace."

So when I show up at the pool I have an eight-year-old in tow, swinging his goggles like a lasso.

"I'm so sorry," I say to Danny. "It's just that Mum's…" What? Having one of her moments? One of her days, weeks, months? I can't tell him that. "She's busy in the kitchen and she can't watch Finn and do that at the same time and I…"

"Hey, hey. Slow down," he says. Then turns. "I'm Danny," he says, holding out a hand.

"Finn," says Finn, shaking it.

"Come on." I tug at Finn's jacket. "We should change." I've done it before, taken him into girls' toilets and stuff.

It's fine. But Danny steps in.

"No, Billie. He can come with me."

"Cool," says Finn, nonchalant. Though I can see he's anything but.

"Er. Well, I'll see you in the pool, then," I say.

"You will," Danny says, and grins.

"You have to kick harder," Finn tells me.

"I know," I protest.

"It's easy, look." He dives underwater, arcing round me like a seal, then bursting through the surface, laughing. And me? I'm just trying to keep my head above the water.

"Ignore him," Danny says. "He'll soon get bored."

And he does. Bored of the big sister who can barely get three strokes without swallowing then coughing up half a pint of chlorine. Bored of Danny, who's too busy helping her to race him.

So Finn huffs off to the deep end to dive, leaving Danny and me floundering in a metre of water.

"Your neck's too stiff," he says.

"I know that," I snap. "How else am I meant to breathe though? I don't want to drown."

"Hey," he says, his voice Luka's, when he's trying to calm Mum, make her see reason. "You won't drown."

"How do you know?"

"Because I won't let you," he replies. "You have to trust me, Billie."

"I do." I relent. "It's just, with Finn—"

"I know. But he's gone now."

I look down to the deep end. See Finn standing on the edge, fingers pointed, face pure concentration. He leaps, a perfect curve, the water barely moving as he plunges beneath the surface. He's a natural. And I am out of my depth.

"There's nothing to be scared of," Danny says.

"I'm not scared," I lie.

"OK. Here's what we're going to do. You're going to hold my hands. And we're going to go underwater. We're not going to swim. We're just going to float. And it doesn't matter if it gets in your eyes or in your mouth. It's water, Billie. Just water."

He's so controlled, so clear, that I don't say anything, just let him take my hands. And on the count of three, he pulls me down.

I thought it would be silent down there. That I would be wrapped in some kind of cocoon, my senses blocked. But I can hear the swirl of water rippling in and out of my ears, the muffled splash of Finn diving, then Danny's voice, a strange alien sound.

I can't work out what he's saying. I open my eyes automatically to lip-read but the chlorine stings and I squeeze them shut again. Should have worn goggles but I was too vain.

My throat is tight. I'm not used to holding my breath like this. I need to surface. But then I feel something against my mouth. Something soft. But alive. It is a kiss. Danny is kissing me.

I don't open my eyes. I don't move. I just let him push his lips onto mine. Let him release a hand so he can touch my face. And it's not how I imagined. Because believe me, I have imagined this now for days: the way he would feel, taste, move; what he would say before and after. It's nothing like any of the pictures I drew in my head. And my lungs are burning because I really need air. But that's not how it feels. It feels right. It feels perfect.

Then he pulls me up, his mouth on mine until the last second. And my feet are on the bottom. And I can breathe.

"What were you doing?" Finn has appeared next to us.

Danny says, "Nothing." But as he holds my gaze, I know it's a lie. It wasn't nothing. It was something. Everything.

ELEANOR

FOUR YEARS ago Eleanor thought he had died. Hoped he had, she remembers with only slight shame. But it was a false alarm. Instead he was retired early on medical grounds, and then it was the two of them. Every day she feeds him, washes him. Reads to him. She remembers Het and Will as babies. Their helplessness. And her responsibility. The day-in-day-out of it all. Is this what we become? she thinks to herself. Babies again?

Every day for four years she nurses him until one morning she takes him a glass of water and he is gone, his face as pale as the sheets he is lying on, the skin already cold. And her heart soars. And when she cries it is not for the loss of him, but for what he has taken from her. She cries for an hour. Then she blows her nose, stands, and calmly calls the hospital.

He is buried a week later. The cemetery chapel is packed. Colleagues cram the pews with their suits and their staidness and their sympathy.

"Whatever will you do without him?" sobs Carol Lister into her monogrammed handkerchief.

Eleanor has an idea.

She wears black for seven days. Then on the eighth, she puts on a yellow sundress, dabs Chanel on her collarbone, and walks down Camborne Hill to the gallery.

BILLIE

"YOU CAN come in."

Finn is looking up at Danny expectantly while my hand hovers with the key half in, half out of the lock.

"You don't have to," I say quickly. Don't want to spoil things. Don't want him to see Mum and run. God knows what she's doing now. Or wearing. It could be anything.

But then the door swings open, disappears from under my fingers, and Mum is standing there. And I can see she's not in a summer dress or her underwear. She's in jeans, red lipstick, and a Cheshire Cat smile. She stares at him for a second, as if she's forgotten who I was with. Then she comes to. "You must be Danny," she says. "Come in."

She sounds normal. Looks normal. But I can tell she's just wearing it. And it doesn't quite fit. It pinches. And I'm scared she'll burst out of it, or take it off.

"No," I say.

But Mum's not taking no for an answer and before I even get inside she's grabbed his hand and virtually yanked him down the hallway, firing questions at him, scatter-gun style.

"So where do you live? How old are you? Would you like cream soda? Or Coke? I have both."

Danny looks back at me, but there's nothing I can do except shrug and follow them in.

Mum makes us Coke floats, the vanilla clouding the syrupy black until it turns to coffee-colour slush. I say nothing. Can't get a word in anyway. Mum is talking nineteen to the dozen. Danny nods, like he knows what she's saying. But he doesn't. Even she doesn't know. And I want to interrupt, to take him upstairs, away from this, from her. But I can't do it now. Because he's made some comment about the piano. About how it's a nice one, and Mum's telling him how she nearly sold it but changed her mind, because every house should have a piano.

And I'm thinking, That's rich, remembering Call-Me-Ken saying we'd have to pay him to take it away, when Danny says, "I play."

And I know it's just polite conversation, that he's just trying to make her feel at ease, but Mum's black kohl-rimmed eyes light up and, "Then you must," she says. "You must play now, for us."

"I—" he begins.

"Can I?" asks Finn. "I can play 'Chopsticks'. Dad taught me."

"Later, bunny," says Mum. And she's practically shoving Danny onto the stool.

Please, God, I think to myself. Please let him be at least a little bit good, because I don't know what she'll say if *he* just does 'Chopsticks' or something. Don't know what I'll say.

And Finn's still begging to have a go and there's all this noise inside and outside my head when he silences me, silences us all. Because it turns out Danny *can* play.

It was his secret, I think. And I wonder why he never told me. Because he's not just Grade-8 good, or school-concert good, he's should-be-going-to-Guildhall-or-the-Royal-Academy good. I listen as the notes pour out of him, watch his fingers tense and relax and tense again, the bones outlined as he spans the keyboard.

And when I look at Mum I can see her eyes are unfocused and a tear is running black Rimmel down her cheek. She's gone.

"Oh, I'm sorry," she says at last. When he's stopped. When I've whispered "Mum?", pulled at her arm, trying to bring her back from wherever it is she's been.

"You play beautifully, Danny," she says. "I was just …

lost in it. The music."

"My turn," Finn demands.

Danny stands to let Finn take his place.

"Mum, watch me," he says and begins to hammer out the idiotic up-and-down cheeriness of 'Chopsticks'.

"Are you watching?" he asks.

"What?" She looks over, sees his concentration, like it's Beethoven's Fifth he's playing, not some nursery Grade 1 practice piece. "Later," she says. "I'm just a bit tired."

She reaches out to the door handle, as if to go. But as she clutches the cut crystal, I can see she is shaking, that the handle is the only thing holding her up.

"I think I need to lie down."

"It was nice to meet you," Danny says.

She turns to him, dazed and confused. "Yes," she says.

"Mum?" I try again.

She clicks back into focus. "I'm just tired," she insists. "I'll be fine in a bit."

But I'm not so sure. Because under the streaks of eye-liner, the sticky pink dust of blusher, her face is white. She looks like a ghost. Or as if she's seen one.

"Who taught you?" I ask.

We've left Finn working his way through a bad rendition of some TV theme tune and are sitting on the edge of my bed. Not because I want us to do anything. At least not right now. But because there's nowhere else to go.

"People," he says. "I mean, my stepdad got me a keyboard. Then I had lessons here and there, when we could afford it."

"You have to do something with it."

"When I have the money, maybe." He looks up at a crack in the plaster. Then turns back. "Anyway, why can't I just do this?"

"Because it's a waste," I say. And I mean it.

"Why do people always say that? Like I'm breaking some law."

"Because you are," I say. "It's wrong to waste stuff."

"Is it?"

I nod.

But he doesn't argue. Instead he kisses me for the second time that day.

This time his lips are warm. And I can taste him now. He is chlorine and Coke and vanilla ice cream. Sweet.

He moves his mouth down the curve of my neck.

"Billie," he breathes, as a hand traces my spine, the fingers finding their way under the thin jersey of my T-shirt.

I feel my heart quickening. And I shudder with want.

But something's wrong.

"Wait." I pull away, breathing hard and fast.

"What is it?"

"Mum. I can't. Not here."

He pauses, looking at me, in me. And then he kisses me again, slowly, softly, on the lips.

"Tomorrow," he says. "Meet me after work."

And I nod. Let his mouth brush the top of my head

before he stands. Then I lie back and listen. Listen to his Converse tread on the stairs, his "Bye" to Finn, the slam of the front door. And to my own heart, singing inside me.

H<u>ET</u>

HET LIES back in the chair and listens. She cannot believe he has never told her, never shown her this before.

Underneath the music she can hear the soft tap of his fingertips on the ivory as they fly up and down the keyboard, seeking out their targets, true every time. Their touch so far from the thud of her and Will practising scales they will never remember or use.

"But how...?" she asks when he's finished.

"What? Because I'm too poor to own a piano? Too stupid?"

"No... I didn't mean..."

But he's laughing. "My dad played. Still does. Only it's in the back room of the Red Lion now, not the front of the Majestic."

"I... I had no idea."

"Why should you?" He shrugs.

She is entranced, overwhelmed by a sudden conviction.

"You should apply to college," she says. "To the Royal Academy."

"I can't read music."

"Then learn," she insists.

But he's shaking his head. "What for? So I can end up down the pub too, banging out Beatles tunes every night? Why can't this be enough?"

"Because it can't be," she says. "It just can't."

He strikes up again. Softer this time. A tune Het recognizes as the theme to a TV programme, though she knows it's a classical piece. Bach, maybe, she thinks. Or Brahms.

She's absorbed by it and by her new idea. So much so that she doesn't hear Will and Jonty come into the room. Doesn't see them until it's too late. Until Will has crooked a finger behind the lid of the piano and pulled it like a trigger, letting the polished mahogany slam down on Tom's fingertips.

"Jesus effing Christ," Tom gasps. His mouth hanging open, hands held out in pain. Het can see the white bar across his knuckles where the wood has hit, can see it turning redder by the second.

"Oh, I am sorry," Will says, his voice dripping with sarcasm. Then he turns to Het. "You know what Father would say though. He'll ruin it playing like that."

And he saunters out, grabbing a handful of peanuts from a cut-glass bowl on the way. Jonty follows, his eyes on Het, his crotch pushing into her as he passes.

"Slumming it," he whispers.

"Go to hell," she says quietly back.

Tom's fingers are fine. No lasting damage, the doctor says. But Tom knows it's a lie. And it's the last time he plays the piano. For Het. For anyone.

BILLIE

MUM IS back to the clattering, a whirl of black-eyed anger around the kitchen. I sit at the table nursing a cup of tea, watching as she smears jam on a cream cracker then throws the sticky knife in the Belfast sink. It misses and hits a half-full glass of red wine, which teeters for a second, then topples, splintering on the hard porcelain, red slopping over the white like a bad scene from *Casualty*.

"Shit," she laments. And then throws out half the cleaning cupboard looking for a dustpan and brush. I should help her, I think. Should do what I always do, enter stage right, the heroine, and clear it up, make it go away, make it better. But I'm distracted. Caught in my own chaos. My own world.

All I can think about is him. The smell of him, the taste of him. The curve of his jaw, his eyelashes long, too long for a boy, but beautiful all the same. The line of his neck; his fingers, deft, taut, as they flicker across ivory. I sketch him in my head, seeing the light and shadows, then on paper, his hair a dark charcoal, his eyes softer, lighter, while I hum to an invisible piano, the tune stuck on REPEAT in my memory.

I am going to show him, I think. He played for me, so I will show him this. My sketch-book. My secret. And so, as I leave for work, I stash the battered pad in my pocket.

But it's not him I tell first. In the end I blurt it out before. To another man. A stranger.

Alexander Shaw watches me as I spray polish on the mantelpiece, dust around the stacked canvases and cut-out prints that take the place of the endless china dogs and photos of beaming grandchildren that fill every other room, to make up for absences. He is here today. Found. Back from wherever he goes inside himself.

My fingers linger on a reproduction of Botticelli's *Venus and Mars*, a shrunken postcard version of the original in the National Gallery. I turn it over automatically. "With love," it reads. "E."

"Stunning, isn't it?" he says.

I jump. "Oh, sorry." I prop it back on the shelf, only succeeding in knocking a Picasso to the floor.

"Sorry," I repeat.

"No matter," he says. "Really. I'm glad someone else appreciates them."

"Were you – are you – a painter?" I correct myself.

"Were. Was." He corrects me back. "I had a gallery. Camborne Hill."

"The Blue Gallery?" I say.

"You know it?"

"Yes." Kind of. I have seen it. Locked up now. A TO LET sign hanging in the window instead of oil and watercolour.

And then I get this idea. This need. To show him. Because he'll understand. He'll get it, get me. And maybe it's like talking to someone in a coma, keeping them aware; maybe it will keep him here and now. And so I say, "Wait a minute," and then run out of the door, his "What for?" following me down the corridor, hanging over the faded lino, unanswered.

"Yours?" he asks.

I nod as he turns the pages, his fingers tracing the charcoal and pencil lines.

"They're just family," I say.

He turns another page.

"That's Finn," I say. "My little brother." And he nods as if he can see this, though there's barely any resemblance at all.

Then I show him Danny. The strong sure lines of his jaw. The full mouth. The eyes that are looking at me. In me.

And maybe he sees it too. Or maybe he is seeing something else from another time. Because he starts and the book slips on the worn material of his trousers and I lean forward to grab it before it falls. As I do, the locket slips forward from under my T-shirt, dangles in front of me, its edges catching the light.

"My God," he says, and he reaches to clasp it. Then before I can stop him he clicks it open.

"My uncle," I say, as he stares at the tiny portrait. "Will. He died."

He nods again. "But where's the other one?"

"What other one?" I ask.

"The girl." He is frantic now. I am losing him. "What was her name?" he demands. "What was it? What was her name?" He searches the air in front of him vainly. Looking for a memory, a ghost.

"I – I don't know. Eleanor?" I try.

Then his eyes fix on mine, and I can see he has grasped it, for a second, an insubstantial thing, a ghost.

"Not Eleanor," he says. "Het."

ELEANOR

HE GIVES her the parcel after work. Upstairs in the studio, amongst the stacked canvases and jars of brushes and smell of oil paint and gouache. Upstairs, where no one can see them: their anticipation, their trepidation.

She opens it with trembling fingers. The brown paper cut with his scalpel and fastened with masking tape; sheep's clothing, disguising the wolf inside.

Eleanor feels her heart beating in her chest. For it is a wolf. A jeweller's box. She holds it still for a second, scared of what it might reveal. And when she looks up and meets his eyes, she sees the same fear and hope reflected back at her. He nods at her to open it. To step into the unknown.

She steels herself and lifts the tautly hinged lid. There,

nestled on claret-coloured velvet, is a fat, flat lozenge of silver. A locket.

She feels herself gasp and turns to him again. "I—"

But he knows what she is going to say. That she can't. That they can't. And he cuts her off. "Take it," he says. "It's yours. Say you bought it. Say you found it. Say anything. But please, keep it."

"What do I put in it?" she asks. "Who do I put in it?"

"Children," he says. "When they come."

"Will they come?"

But she knows the answer before he says it. "Of course they will."

She starts to speak again but cannot find the words.

"Here," he says. And from her shaking hands he lifts out the pendant on its gossamer thread, undoes the clasp.

"Turn around," he says.

And she does, and sees the fine chain in his calloused fingers, sees the locket catch the sunlight from the wide studio windows, a sudden flash of white in her eyes, feels his hands at the back of her neck, his warm breath as deep and fast as her heartbeats, the cold metallic hardness of the pendant against her ribcage.

"There."

She turns and he takes her in his arms. And, for the first time, they kiss.

The locket is the start of it all, and the end.

* * *

She tells Roger she bought it with her wages. That it is a treat to herself.

He nods, says nothing. But later, when he checks the account, he can find no receipt. And then snatches of gossip make their way to the hospital.

That Carol Lister admired the locket on Eleanor, asked her where she had got it. That Harry White the jeweller told Carol he had only ever had one as she described, and he sold it not to Eleanor but to that artist, what was his name? Shaw, that was it. Shaw. That Carol told her husband, said she was certain it was only a mix-up, and that she wasn't one to cast aspersions, but that it did seem, well, odd.

Three weeks later it is over. They are over.

Roger is consumed with anger. His eyes black with it, his words sharp. He orders her to leave her job. To say she wants to concentrate on a family now. Because appearances must be kept up, no matter what the Listers know.

She does as he tells her. Though it breaks her heart. She gives it up, gives him up. Lets the door close, and walks up the hill, breathing her last gasps of freedom, of hope, before shutting herself into the stifling binds of Cliff House.

She will see him in town, on the beach, say hello. But nothing more. Not now.

But the locket she keeps. Shut away in a drawer in her dresser. A thing of secrets. Of hopes.

When he is out, she sits, takes it from its keeping place,

and holds its flat smoothness in her palm.

"One day," she thinks. And she places it against her gently swelling belly. "One day."

BILLIE

I GO to Danny's flat from work. Tell him what Alexander has said. Ask him what it means.

But Danny says it's nothing, that Alex is just confused. That he's seen it with his nan. That once she thought he was his dead uncle, once his grandad.

And I nod, believe him, because I want the words to stop, want our lips to cut them off. And they do. He kisses me and I feel the questions dissolve, because all that matters, all that I need to be sure about, is here. And I am sure. I am so sure.

It's late now. Dark. We're at the door. My face stinging from his stubble, my stomach empty. So lost in each other we forgot to eat.

"I'll walk you home," he says, reaching for his coat.

Part of me wants to say yes, wants to keep him close for as long as I can, wants to feed off this feeling. But it's what's at the other end I'm scared of. And I want this to be ours for as long as possible. Our secret.

"No, you're all right," I say. "This isn't Peckham." Thank God.

"Are you sure?"

"Sure I'm sure."

"Can I see you tomorrow?"

"I'm working."

"Playing hard to get?"

I laugh. "No, really, I am." I pull a face, then he pulls me to him, kisses me hard.

"I'll call you," he breathes when I break away.

"Yeah. No— wait. You can't. The phone's broken." Bloody Mum.

"So find me then," he says.

"I will," I say. I will. And I kiss him one last time before I go.

I walk home slowly, taking the long route along the seafront, delaying the inevitable. The banging and the whirling. Finn's had it all day. He just ignores her. Takes his chance to watch what he likes and eat what he likes.

When I reach the pier I stop. Something's different. There's a smell of petrol, of oil generators mixing with salt and burgers. It is a smell of hope. Of life.

The fair is coming alive.

And suddenly I see that picture postcard, see the promise of everything this place could be, fulfilled. Sun, sand, the fairground. And Danny. And I laugh. Because in that instant my world is perfect. I have everything. Even without my father. I have it all.

But I've forgotten about Mum.

I can hear it before I even get to the gate: the muffled distortion of a stereo on at full volume. When I open the door I am deafened by it. The sound of late-night radio, of the obscure blues and soul that Mum loves. I slam the door behind me and race to the drawing room, thanking God, or my grandparents, that the house is detached, that there's no Mrs Hooton standing on the doorstep complaining that Mum won't answer, that it's been like this for hours, that she's going to call the police if it doesn't stop.

I flick off the power and look around for someone to shout at. But there's no one. Finn has somehow slept through it all. And Mum? She's in the kitchen. Asleep too. A glass of something pale and alcoholic in front of her. I sniff it and gag. It's strong. Strong enough to block out the sound of Etta James, and whatever it is that's haunting her. The ghosts that are beginning to haunt me.

I rinse the glass under the tap, put it away. But Mum I can't move. She's too heavy, the drink seems to add stones to her. I decide to leave her. Switch off the lights.

But as I turn to go I hear the swish of paper skimming

across the floor. Something has fallen from Mum's lap. I stoop to pick it up and see the familiar red ink. Bills. Not just one. A whole pile of them. I gather them up and put them in the cupboard, next to the coffee jar. They can wait until morning too.

Het

HET IS *in the bath, her ten-year-old legs rippling in a ruler-deep pool, like they're made of aspic not flesh. She pokes a big toe inside the tap. To see if it still fits. It does. And she leaves it there, the metal gripping it, her head pushed hard back against the white enamel. Until the water is cold, until her body shrivels and the toe drops out of the tap, back into the water.*

Then, eyes still staring at the gloss-painted ceiling, Het lets her knees rise up and her head slide down and under.

She holds her breath. Until the faint, blurred dripping becomes a whooshing, banging of blood in her ears. Until the forty-watt light bulb becomes a thousand-kilowatt sun, bursting into fireworks across her retinas. Until she feels two hands

*grasp her arms and yank her up into the air, shake her like a
doll, crying her name.*

"Hetty! Hetty!"

It is her mother.

Het's eyes pull into focus.

"Hello," she says.

*Her mother lets her drop and Het's bottom hits the bath
with a thud, bruising her and sending a tidal wave over
the rim.*

*Her mother is shaking. "You silly girl. What in God's
name do you think you were doing?"*

"Practising," she replies.

"What for?"

*Het looks at her mother as if she is the one who is mad.
"For being dead, of course."*

BILLIE

WHEN I go downstairs the next morning Mum is still at the kitchen table, but awake now, the radio back on and a cup of black coffee in her hand.

I open the plate cupboard, check the top shelf. They're still there: the sheets of red-inked paper, shouting our last-chance warnings.

It's worse than I imagined. The gas alone is over five hundred pounds. That's more than we got through in a year in London. But then we weren't living in some five-bedroomed fairy-tale palace.

"When did these come?" I ask her.

She shrugs. "I don't know."

"Are there others?"

She doesn't even bother to lie or argue. She's too tired. "In the knife drawer."

I pull at the chrome handle and slide the drawer out. There should be ominous music, I think. Like one of those shlock horror films where you want to scream at the TV, "Don't open the door!" But instead some song on the radio keeps telling me to smile. Yeah, right.

We owe over three thousand pounds. Gas, electricity, some credit card that I didn't even know she had, a tab from Aladdin's Cave, which explains how she's been getting the drink and the cigarettes and the olives and cake. And a letter from some solicitors chasing two thousand pounds in back rent for Mr Garroway.

My stomach beats alive with wings as I remember the postcard I sent Luka. No envelope. Just our address in inky capitals, shouting our hiding place.

I am an idiot. And we are screwed. We can never find that kind of money. Not without selling the house. Unless…

I remember what Mum said. That my grandparents must have had other money, not just the house. And somewhere there must be records of that. I don't remember Mum throwing out any papers or getting rid of any box files, so they must still be here.

I start in the kitchen, going through all the drawers and cupboards. But there's nothing. Just apple-corers and tin-openers and other metal objects that look like instruments of torture.

"What are you doing?" Mum asks.

"Nothing," I say. "Well, maybe something. I don't know."

She doesn't reply. Just stares into the bottom of her coffee cup looking for God knows what. Hope. Inspiration. The secret of the universe.

I go to the dining room next. The mahogany dresser. The shelves have been cleared of crystal paperweights and silver salvers but underneath the cupboards are crammed with paper and folders and files. Billie Paradise: *dix points*.

I'm not sure what it is I'm looking for, but I figure I'll know when I see it. A will, or insurance documents, or bank statements, or something. I can hear Cass in my head: "Oh My God, it's totally like *CSI*. You are so the one with the accent and the legs." And I laugh. But it's not funny; it's so far from funny.

It's not there. But I find something else. Something that makes me forget about the bills, and the money.

It's at the bottom of a drawer. A grey cardboard file, with a single word on the cover, in blue-black ink, the *l*s in loops, alive. It says, "Will".

Inside are more certificates, too many to hang on the walls, letters of commendation, school reports, *A*s and *B*s from English to Latin. No "Could do better"s. No "Not performing to the best of her ability"s that dotted mine and littered Cass's.

I read the newspaper cuttings. Rowing competitions, rugby tournaments, and him, always him, his name in lights, his face black and white but coloured with pride.

Somehow, this flimsy cardboard contains him. This strong, substantial, incredible boy. Full of promise, of life.

Then I find it. The last cutting. No smiling headshot, no glowing headline. Instead, four short printed words shout out what I knew, and what I didn't. "YOUNG RUGBY STAR DROWNS."

I feel dizzy. Weak. As if the words have sent me spinning like a top. Because it wasn't a disease, wasn't a car crash. The things I'd wondered, imagined. He fell from the pier and drowned. And I remember that night, the first night with Danny. On the end of the boardwalk with Eva and Mercy. Remember Jake grabbing me, the water beneath us, and the story they told. About the undertow, about how it pulled you down, that you couldn't fight it.

And then I know why Mum stays away. Why she's so scared of even the swimming-pool. Because of this. Because it was the water that killed her brother.

ELEANOR

IT HAS *been two days when the policeman finally calls. Two days of hand-wringing silence and Carol fussing with sweet tea and sour gin.*

Roger answers the door; Eleanor's legs are too weak, her voice long gone.

The policeman is young, Eleanor thinks, too young to be the detective that his stripes proclaim. Too young to speak these words, to bear this news. Not much older than Will.

He sits awkwardly on the wingback chair, waiting for the cup of tea that Carol insists on making before finally telling her what she has been expecting, dreading.

"We've found a body," he says.

* * *

A body, not a boy. That is all he is now. Muscle and sinew and skin. Laid out on a slab in the same hospital that his father works in.

They bury him a week later. Close the door to his room. Place the file in the drawer and push it shut. Ephemera. It is nothing. Not the essence of him. Just things.

But his ghost. His ghost will haunt them for ever.

BILLIE

I **PHONE** in sick to work. Say I've got some viral thing. Debs swears. Says now she's going to have to do a double-shift because Lisa's still off. For a second I think I'll change my mind. Because God knows we need the money. But I need this more.

Mum is still holding the cup of coffee, stone-cold now. As I walk in she looks up and I see the dark circles under her eyes. Heroin chic. Not.

"Where are you going?" Her voice is tinged with something. Worry? Panic?

"Just out." It's no use talking to her about it. Not with the way she is. She'll only cry. Or worse.

She puts down the cup, stands suddenly, the chair

clattering on the floor as she reaches to hold my arms in her white fingers. "With Danny?"

I can't do this now. Can't do the "Be careful, you're only young, look what happened to me" thing.

"He's just a friend," I assure her. "OK?" I take her arms and put them down at her sides. "That's all. A friend. You don't need to worry. It's fine. I'm fine."

"A friend," she repeats. "OK."

"I have to go, Mum," I say. And I kiss her on the cheek, and leave her, wrapped in the quiet chaos of her own world.

But as I get to the door I realize I have no idea where I'm going or how to get there.

So I do what any damsel in distress does. Find a knight in shining armour.

"The cemetery," he says. "Pensilva."

I nod. Of course. "You know where it is?"

He breathes out heavily. "Yeah."

"Is it weird to want to see him? See them?" I ask. "Like, wrong?"

"No." Danny shakes his head. "It's closure. Isn't that what they call it?"

"Yeah." And I see Martha in her mirrored skirts, putting on her fake German accent but meaning it anyway as she begged Mum to call Eleanor, to have it out with her. To get closure.

"Oh Billie, I'm so sorry," he says.

"I knew he was dead," I say. "It's not like it was a

surprise. But it's made it real somehow. Made him real. Do you see?"

And he does. Of course he does.

He borrows Jake's van and we drive there in silence. When we stop, get out onto the rain-soaked sand of the car park, he reaches for my hand, keeps it in his until we find them.

They're side by side. Three of them. Eleanor, Roger and William. Like the Three Bears. Or Three Wise Monkeys. Speak no evil. Their lives and deaths etched in pink-brown quartz, flecked with silver scales. Like salmon, I think. And I try to smile, but instead the tears come, and they don't stop. I kneel on the damp ground, my hands deep in the cold soil of the graves, and I cry for their loss, and for mine. For the memories we never shared, for the hours, days, weeks spent in our own worlds, when we could have been in each other's.

I cry until the rain starts to drip its steady suffering, until Danny pulls me up and to him, tells me we need to go, that it's late, that he has to get the van back.

"I don't need to go, though," he says, his lips warm against my neck. "I could come back with you. Or we could go out. Do something. Swim, even?"

But I don't want the muffled weight of water pulling me under. I want clarity, light. I want to be up in the air. I want to fly. Want to feel drunk and dizzy and dazed and anything, anything but this. I tilt my head back, let Danny pull damp strands of hair away from my eyes.

"Take me to the fair," I plead. "Will you? Will you take me to the fair?"

HET

HET CALLS home. *Two weeks after they find Will's body in the water. Two days after they find Tom's.*

She swore to Martha that she wouldn't, that she didn't care what they thought of her. And it was true, of him. But her mother... She thinks of her in that house with him, remembers her sitting at the dressing-table, the veins in her throat taut with worry, with sadness. Feels the life inside her. Filling her with hope. Hope she wants to share, has to share, despite everything that has gone before.

"Mother?" she says, carefully, quietly.

"Het? Oh Het."

She can hear relief flood her mother's voice in the space of three words. But then she hears something else. The clatter of a receiver being dropped, and then a rasp of heavy breath as it is picked up again. Breath that smells of whiskey and Hamlets.

"They're dead," the voice says. "Do you hear me? Dead."

Het feels the ground give way underneath her. She sinks into a beanbag, sending tiny pearls of polystyrene skittering across the floorboards.

"Who—? Who is dead?" she asks.

"Your brother. And that boy. He killed him. Hit Jonty. Killed Will. Pushed him off the pier. Jonty saw it. Saw it all."

Het can't keep it down. She bolts to the bathroom and heaves up a string of vomit and with it a great screaming cry of pain.

When she picks up the receiver again she hears a click and then the dialling tone. It is the last time she will ever speak to them.

BILLIE

I **WANT** to be taken away. And the fair is another world. Swarming and bright and loud; the music pumping so hard I can feel it in my chest. Half real, half fantasy. Or freak show. Where hard white sugar can be spun into soft pink peaks, where you can watch yourself morph from a giant into Rumpelstiltskin, and where you can lose yourself in the crowds and the smell and the noise.

And I do. I ride rockets and the octopus and the waltzers, trying to lose me, lose Will, lose Eleanor and all of them, to spin and speed them out of me.

We're stumbling off the cakewalk, giddy with it, when Danny stops suddenly, letting go of my hand so that I pitch forward and knock into some girl in a hoodie who swears as Cherry Coke sloshes over her hand and gives me a hard-as-nails, hard-as-Cass stare.

"Sorry. I'm sorry." I turn to Danny. But he's not looking at me. He's staring at this guy on the goldfish stall. This tall, dark man, who has Danny's eyes, and height, and that slow, lazy smile.

And it hits me like a slew of rainwater. Cold and shocking. Waking me from the dream I'm trying to find my way back to. Because I know in that second who he is. He is Danny's father. An overgrown version of the boy at my side, a hall-of-mirrors man, talking the talk, swapping gold coins for darts, without taking his eyes off Danny for a second.

I reach for Danny's arm, hold it, run my hand down to his.

"We should go," he says.

I don't get it. "Don't you want to, I don't know … say hello?"

Danny shakes his head. "Not now."

And then I do. I get it. That nothing's ever easy. Families are never easy. Not mine with no dad, no money and Mum on another planet. Not Danny's with his mum gone to a cosy new semi-detached life and this half-stranger riding in for a few weeks a year like some cowboy. Not Cass's. Not Eva's. No one's.

"Let's go to yours," I say.

As we walk away, out of this Neverland, I glance over my shoulder, catch him watching us through the crowd. He's got this look on his face. This "Who are you, kid?"

look. The same look I got from Eva. From Debs. From the guy in the Internet café. But for once it doesn't freak me out. Or piss me off. Because I know who I am. Who I want to be. Tonight, at least.

I want to be Danny's.

We're in his bedroom. Eva and Jake next door, arguing over something and nothing.

"He was never my dad," Danny says, his fingers tracing a pattern on the duvet, his eyes watching the fast movements. "Not really. Not like he changed a nappy when he was here. Or sent a birthday card when he wasn't. Just a bloke, really. A bloke who slept with my mum." I touch his face, and his eyes flick up and meet mine. "We're the same," he says. "You and me."

"The same," I repeat.

He looks at me, into me. And as we kiss, I know it is true. That I am him. He is me. We are each other.

"Stay," he says. And I could, I think. Could stay in this little room, with the sea outside the window and the curtains that don't close and the half-hearted two-bar heater. Could fall asleep, with his chin against my shoulder, his arms round mine, our bodies locked like a Chinese puzzle. But...

"I can't," I say. "Mum."

"Not that," he says. "I mean here, in Seaton. Don't go. Ever."

"But what about college?" I ask. "I thought—"

"It can wait. Until you can go. Until—"

And I kiss him my answer. Because I am surer than ever. That I want to be here. In this rain-sodden granite-grey dead-end town. I don't want to go back to London. Don't want to spend another Saturday night standing outside Magic City with a bottle of Breezer in my hand and Cass's borrowed shoes pinching my toes and her laugh digging at my heart.

I want to stay. I want to be with him. For ever.

HET

"**HAVE YOU**...? I mean, have you done this before?"

Het shakes her head, and drops it, half proud that at nineteen she is a virgin. Despite Jonty's pushing insistence. Despite the pleas and the threats. Half ashamed that she has no idea what to do. And that he does. She knows that there have been others. Kelly. Maybe that other girl too. She remembers the glittered lettering on the back of her top. Debs. That was it.

Tom lifts her chin, places his fingers against her cheek. "It doesn't matter," he says. "None of it, none of what's gone before."

Then he pulls her gently to him, and kisses her.

* * *

Afterwards they lie silently in the dark, their arms still holding the other, legs entwined; like a strange two-headed creature, she thinks.

"I love you," he whispers into her hair.

And Het smiles, not just because of these three small words, but because, instead of emptiness, her heart is full, full to bursting.

BILLIE

I COME downstairs the next morning to find Mum eating cornflakes out of the packet like crisps. And I know that I can't tell her about Will yet. About the folder. Or about Danny. The way I feel about him. The way he makes me feel. I know that I'm going to have to bury more secrets like beating tell-tale hearts.

But I have to tell her something. I have to do something to keep us here. Me here, with Danny. So I send Finn up to change his Batman pyjamas that he's been in for two days. Tell him to shower, to clean his teeth.

"You're not my mum," he says. But even he knows that, right now, that's exactly who I am.

So I sit down and do what I think a mum should do.

I take her hand in mine and I tell her something. The only bit she needs to know right now. That we can't afford to live here. That we have to sell it. Find somewhere smaller. Cheaper. With windows that keep the rain out and the heat in.

And I wait for her to shoot back. To tell me I'm talking rubbish. That we're millionaires. That we can live on cornflakes and shortbread. But instead, she just squeezes my hand weakly, then pulls her own away.

"I'll ask the estate agent to come, then," I say. "To value it, I mean. I can go on the way to work."

I look at her. At her face, pale and taut across her cheekbones, the skin grey. Her fingers shaking as she reaches inside the cellophane for another mouthful of cereal. And I know it's not just an estate agent I need.

"I'll call the doctor, too."

That's when she shoots. Her hand cracking on the table like a single gunshot. And a single word. "No."

"Bu—"

"I'm fine," she says. "I'm tired, that's all. Tired. Not a bloody loony tune. Christ, Billie. See the estate agent, OK? Just do it."

She stands and slams the cereal on the counter. Grabs the kettle and fills it noisily, the tap on too hard so the water ricochets off and soaks the tiles and her dress. She jumps back and drops the kettle in the sink. "Shit."

"Mum?"

She raises one hand to her face, grasps the elbow with

her other. And she starts shaking, her head bobbing up and down unevenly, gasps of breath sounding in time with the clock. It's not until she turns to me that I see that the gasps aren't tears, that the shaking isn't her all racked with sorrow. It's laughter. She is laughing.

"I'm sorry," she pants.

"What happened?" Finn is back. Unshowered, but in clean clothes at least.

"Nothing, baby," Mum says quickly. "I just had a little accident."

"Ugh," he says, looking at the darkening stain on her dress.

"Oh. God. No!" she says. "Not that. The tap. I was just—" But she's off again. Laughing. Finn with her. Then she turns the tap on and they've got glasses and they're throwing water over each other, over the table, the floor.

But not over me. I leave them to it and walk down the hill to town.

I expected the estate agent to be some fat cat in a pinstripe suit. Like the wide boys in Peckham, driving X5s and stinking of Versace, their blakeys tapping along the high street. But he's not. He's this thin, mousy, middle-aged man in a beige shirt and brown tie. Like he wants to disappear into the studded walls behind him.

"I need proof of ownership," he says, like I knew he would. Because how often do sixteen-year-olds tell you they want to sell the family estate. So I hand him the title deeds and the letter. The one I got that day back at the flat, wrapped around the magic key. Not so magic now.

Except for Danny.

"Are you looking to move within the area?" he says.

"I…" I realize I haven't asked Mum. Or told her. What if she wants to go back? Or needs to go back? If the ghosts are what's killing her? But I can't. I have to find a way. "I think so," I say. "Yes. Yes I am— We are."

"Well, here." He hands me a wodge of papers; details of terraces and bungalows. Ones like Eva's. Tight rows, opening out on to the street. No long gardens, no gates, no drawbridges. No more castles. That fairy tale is over.

"Thanks," I say. "I'll give them to my mum."

But I won't. I push them inside the ripped pocket of the Burberry. With twenty pence and a half-chewed piece of juicy fruit wrapped up in silver foil. And later I'll put them under my bed, or in a drawer. Where she can't find them. Not yet.

"So, just some twenty-four-hour thing was it?"

I nod.

Debs is outside the Laurels, a ciggie hanging on her lower lip while she talks, the smoke curling past the creases of her lips, up into the bleach of her hair. I wonder how old she is. Maybe the same as Mum. But she looks a decade more.

"You're not supposed to be back for two days," she says. "Case you give it to 'em in there." She gestures behind her.

"But I—"

"Oh, it's all right. I don't give a monkey's. As long as no one's puking tomorrow. 'Cause if they are, it'll be you clearing it up."

I'm not sure if she's joking, so I don't say anything. Just turn and walk up the steps, push open the double doors, feel the blast of hot air and the smell of Irish stew.

The thing is, I want to work. Need to work. For the money, and the monotony. I need to do something. Or I'll think about Will. And Mum. Be consumed by it. The awfulness and waste of it all.

I scrub tiles until my nails break the thin pink rubber of the Marigolds, until I can feel the Dettol-rich water soak into my fingertips, trickle up my arm. I vacuum invisible crumbs and cotton threads. And I lose myself in it, and in him.

I'm in Alex's room, cleaning the toilet, when I hear his voice behind me.

"I never said I was sorry."

I jump. Look up from the cracked porcelain of the toilet bowl I've been wiping to see him standing in the doorway.

"God, I—" I stand awkwardly. "Pardon? What did you say?"

"I'm sorry. About Will."

I remember now. The locket. I clutch it automatically.

"It was a terrible business," he says. "Terrible."

"He drowned," I say. "I know. I found out."

"Both of them," he adds. "Him and that other boy."

He's pulling on the bottom button of his cardigan, a wooden toggle, like on a kid's duffel coat.

I feel cold creep down my spine like the legs of a spider. "What other one?" I say. Not Jonty. Because he rang. He is alive.

"Found him two weeks later. Two weeks in the water, can you imagine?"

I feel the butterflies coming to life. "Who was in the water?" I ask slowly. "What was his name?"

"His name?" he mutters to himself. And then he bangs the flat of his hand on his forehead. "Can't remember," he repeats. "Can't." He is pulling the toggle harder and harder, and I think the wool tying it is about to snap. But something else does.

"Who was he?" I plead, the butterflies frantic now. "Who died?"

He lets go of the toggle and looks at me, shock spreading across the creased map of his face.

"Your daddy, Billie. Your daddy, of course."

JONTY

IT IS dark when Jonty wakes. Pitch-black. The lights from the fair long extinguished. It takes him four breaths to work out where he is, longer to stand, his brain dulled by alcohol, his legs aching with cold.

He holds on to the railing, keeping himself upright against the wind and his own stomach and head, which will him back down with every second. But he mustn't listen. Because he remembers now. Remembers what happened.

Remembers the Gypsy boy, Het's boy, shouting. Remembers Will's hands slamming into his shoulders. Pushing him. Then the water. The water. He remembers Will, his head going under, then back up, his mouth gaping like a fish. Then he is gone. He stares down into the inky depths. There is nothing there. Just *the vastness of the sea. Miles wide and fathoms deep. Did he come out? It is all too blurred, fuzzy at the edges.*

His stomach contracts violently and he pukes into the darkness below. Then wipes his mouth, turns and lurches home.

In the morning he tells the police what happened. Says the Gyppo pushed Will into the water. Says he had it in for them. Had done for weeks. Says it was over Het. And the baby. That he wanted her to run off with him. Join some Travellers' thing. Will begged him not to. But the Gyppo wasn't having any of it.

He says he saw it all. Says the Gyppo hit him too, knocked him out against the railing. Shows them the bruise on the side of his face.

"Looks to be harder than a fist done that," one officer says.

"He knew what he was doing," says Jonty. "They're all fighters, that sort."

Carol lets out a sob, and Eleanor, who wishes – hopes – her own boy escaped with just a bruise, lays a shaking hand on her shoulder.

"And you'd stand up in court?" says the other officer. The taller one. "Tell them exactly what happened?"

Jonty nods. Cross my heart and hope to die. Stick a needle in my eye.

"You have to be sure," says Eleanor.

"He is," her husband snaps. "For God's sake, woman. He saw it."

* * *

But two weeks later they find him: the Gypsy. Tom. And the morning after, Jonty wakes in a sweat. He has had a dream. A terrible dream, where Tom's hand isn't a fist raised in anger; it is an open palm reaching to help. Where Will isn't pushed; he falls. Where Tom doesn't fall; he jumps. Jumps in to save Will.

But it isn't a dream. It isn't a dream at all.

He goes to his father's study, closes the door, and, with his eyes to the ground, his words faltering, stomach turning, he tells him what he has remembered.

At the grim end, he looks up and waits. Waits for the rage and the fury, for the call to the police, for the sorry confession, and the punishment.

But instead his father says, "It will do no good."

"Pardon?" Jonty feels that in his shaken state he must have misheard. That he is conjuring up what he has willed like a rabbit out of a hat.

But it is no cheap trick.

"They're both dead," he explains. "There will be no prosecution. The truth cannot save the boy. Let Roger and Eleanor believe the best of William. Let it rest."

And he tries. He puts the thought away, buries it under his A levels and medical school and his job at the hospital. He stitches new life into people, trying to make up for the two lost ones, trying to hide the truth.

But when he closes his eyes it pushes its way to the surface, grabs hold of him and pulls him back. To the pier. To that night. And it eats away at him like the blackened cancer he cuts out.

BILLIE

I LEAVE the Laurels with no explanation. No apology. Still in my overall I walk, through metres and metres, hope after hope, dream after dream. Through every "What could have been", every face in the crowd that I imagined was him. She must have known, I think. Must have known he was dead. And all these years I've wasted my time imagining, waiting to meet this man who is no more than a body. A corpse.

And inside I feel the insects batter. But not in fear now. In rage.

I leave the door open behind me, feet trailing mud and leaves and dog shit along the carpet.

She's in the drawing room. In some black ballgown, a glass of wine in her hand. Red, like blood.

"Why didn't you tell me?" I say slowly.

"What?" she turns, spilling wine down her dress, drops staining the carpet, oblivious.

"Why didn't you tell me about my dad?" My words are measured. Cold.

"What?" She tries to laugh it off. "What are you talking about?"

The hollow laughter pokes me, stings me, and I stare angrily at her, breath coming hard now, blood singing in my ears. "All these years… You said he was gone. Gone away. And now I've found out that he's dead. That my dad's dead."

Her face is ashen now. "Oh Billie." The glass tumbles from her hands and hits the carpet as she reaches out to hold me.

And then I know it's true. I slap her arms away. "What happened?" I yell. "I need to know. I need the truth."

Mum shakes her head. "I can't."

"You have to," I bawl. "All these years you've been lying. Now you have to tell me the truth. Tell me the truth," I demand. "Tell me…"

And I repeat it, banging out the words like a rhythm on a drum, until she puts her hands over her ears and screams out, "He killed him."

The words plunge into me, a blade. I gasp. "What?"

She claps a hand over her mouth and stares at me in shock. But it's too late. The secret is out.

I grab her arms, shake her like a rag doll. "What do you mean? Who did he kill? What happened?"

"Billie," she pleads.

"Just tell me." I shake her hard again and I feel her go limp.

She looks at me, helpless now. A thing of pity. Hair stuck to her face with snot and tears, her body shaking. She manages to speak through the sobs. "I don't know it all," she says. "Just that there was a fight."

"Who?" I demand. "Who was fighting?"

"Tom – your dad. He hit Jonty, I think."

"And then?"

She lets her head fall and makes a keening sound, like an animal. "Don't make me, Billie."

The noise is pain. And it hurts me too. But I won't stop. Can't stop. "You have to," I spit. "You have to tell me."

And she does. "He hit Jonty," she wails, "and then he pushed Will off the pier."

The butterflies inside me take flight. I feel them rise in my throat. Pushing out a "No". But even as I utter it I know it is hopeless.

"I'm sorry," she cries. "I'm so sorry."

And we're both crying. Me propping her up with my hands, but I can't hold her. Can't be held.

"How?" I manage.

But she shakes her head. "I wasn't there. They told me. He told me."

"Your father?"

She nods. Pulls her head back up so her red-rimmed eyes meet mine. "It was over me," she says. "The fight. Do you understand, Billie? It was my fault. That Will died. That your dad—"

I've heard enough. I let go of her arms and she crumples into a chair, sobbing out more apologies.

But *sorry* isn't what I need. *Sorry* won't change the fact that Tom wasn't brave, or just a coward who never wanted kids.

He was a killer.

JIMMY

IT TAKES *two weeks for Tom's body to come to shore. Blue-lipped and bloated, it catches in the anchor rope of the* Amelia *in a harbour twenty miles down the coast from Seaton. At first the owner thinks it's a dolphin, so pale and cyanotic. But then the tide swells, bobbing the lifeless corpse up to the surface for a second, and instead of fins he sees fingers, and he knows it is a man.*

Jimmy identifies the body. Laid out on cold metal in the basement of the hospital, the fluorescent lights tingeing his skin an impossible green, water still swelling his flesh so that he looks less like a man than a monster: the Incredible Hulk. But even through his Marvel disguise, Jimmy can see it is him. Can see where the toy car cut his forehead. Can see the hands that together span three octaves. The mouth that turns up slowly into a lazy smile. The same mouth as their father. As his own son.

A week later they bury the body. And a week after that Jimmy leaves Seaton: leaves his girlfriend, leaves the little boy with the lazy smile, and doesn't come back for seven years.

BILLIE

MUM IS balled in the armchair, her arms tight around her legs, her body still shaking with tears. I feel weak with it, too. Dizzy. But I can't curl up. Can't give in to it. Because I need to know more. Because she has told me what he was.

But not who. Or why.

And she wasn't there. So how can she know for sure?

I look frantically round the drawing room. At the books. The files. I pull them off the shelves. Shaking them. Trying to find where Eleanor has hidden the rest of the secret. Where she has buried it. Waiting for a slip of paper to fall out.

But there is nothing. Of course there is nothing. Because it isn't her secret to keep. Because she wasn't there either.

But Jonty was. Jonty saw it all. And Jonty didn't crash

his car. Jonty didn't drown. Jonty called the house just days ago.

Jonty is alive.

And then I see it. See Mum stamping on the answerphone. Broken black plastic shards I swept up weeks since. And something else. The handset on the polished table. Still displaying a signal. Which means…

I run to the hall and pick it up and dial 1471.

The number is local, the same code as ours, as Danny's. I punch in "3" and listen as the line connects.

"Dr Lister."

I falter for a second, thrown by the title. But it is him. The same voice, thick with money and class.

"I— My name's Billie—" and I am about to say "Paradise", when I change my mind, remember who I am— "Billie Trevelyan," I say.

"You're—"

"Het's daughter."

There's silence. And I'm scared he is going to hang up. That he changed his mind. That whatever he wanted to say to Mum can stay buried. But I can't let it. I need to speak to him. To see him. "Can you meet me?" I say.

"Of course. I—"

"Do you know Jeanie's?" I interrupt. "It's a café on the seafront."

"Yes. Yes I do. When?"

And I know he's expecting a "tomorrow". Or "in a week". But it can't wait. For either of us.

"Now," I say. "I need to meet now."

The café is empty. A SORRY WE'RE CLOSED sign hanging lopsided in the glass. But the lights are on, and I can hear music filtering out. Not Beyoncé. Guitars. And I feel a surge of relief that it's him.

I knock hard on the window and see him turn, and turn off the radio. Then, wiping his washing-wet hands on an apron, he walks to the door and unlocks it. His eyes on mine the whole time.

"Billie? What's going on?"

I fall into his arms, clutch on to him. The only steady thing I have. The only real thing.

"It's Tom," I say. "My dad… I know what happened."

I tell him what they have told me – Alex and Mum. The fight. That he pushed Will. That they both drowned. But that Jonty saw it. That Jonty is coming.

He says nothing. Just holds me tight to him, so I breathe through the thick checked flannel of his shirt, breathe in the smell of sweat and bacon fat, and peace, and love.

And I want time to stop right then. Want the world to end with just this fleeting sense of serenity. But the clock doesn't stop. The seconds still tick around.

* * *

There is a sharp rap at the door and I look up from Danny's shoulder through the glass, pull away from him, and go to answer it.

The man on the other side is tall, still ruddy-cheeked and blond, like the photograph. But his face and hair have thinned and faint shadows show under his eyes.

"Billie?"

"Yes I— This is Danny."

Jonty nods at him, then surveys the room. The shabbiness of it. Probably used to bars, I think. Country clubs. Not this. But this is where I feel safe. This is where I belong.

"Do you want tea?" Danny asks.

I shake my head. Can't drink. Can barely swallow. Jonty reaches in his pocket and pulls out a silver hip flask. "If you don't mind?" he says.

I shrug, and Danny reaches for a tumbler from behind the counter, hands it to him. Then turns to head into the galley kitchen.

I feel a wave of panic and blurt out, "Stay."

But he won't. "This is family stuff, Billie," he says. "Private stuff. You need to do this by yourself."

"But—"

"It's OK." He reaches for my hand. Squeezes it tight. So tight it almost hurts. But I need it. Need to know he's not lying when he says, "I'm not going anywhere."

"Shall we?" Jonty indicates a table. Eva's table.

I nod, and we sit. Me with my back to the wall, my

hands under my thighs. Hiding the tremors that betray how terrified I am.

Jonty doesn't sit on his hands. Jonty has something else. He unscrews the cap from the flask and pours an inch of whiskey into the scratched glass. I can smell it. Its acrid sweetness. He takes a swig then sets it down between us, the fingers of both his hands still touching the glass, still holding on. Courage, I think. That's what it is. That's why Mum does it. Strength when you have nothing, no one.

"So—"

"Billie—"

We both speak at once. And then fall silent. And I cannot find the words, though a hundred questions are clamouring for attention, demanding answers: Why were they there that night? Why were they there at all? What was he to them? To Mum? How did it start? How did it end?

Jonty can see them. The words, trapped inside me. And so he finds a way to coax them out of their hiding place.

"Why don't you tell me what you know?" he says.

"Not much. Just… That you and Will had a fight with Tom. That Tom pushed Will. And they both drowned." My voice cracks and he pushes the whiskey glass towards me. I shake my head and instead will the tears back down.

"Who told you that?" he asks.

"Mum," I reply. "Het."

"She's wrong," he says.

"But she—"

But he holds up a hand to bat away the end of the sentence. He has waited a long time for this. He has to finish.

So he starts.

"They were Traveller kids. Worked the fair. They never liked us and we never liked them. Tom or his brother Jimmy. No reason. Just because of who they were. Who we were."

He pauses, looks at me to see if I am following. I nod, urging him on. Not wanting him to stop.

"Well, mostly we just stayed out of their way. But then Het – your mum – she started seeing the younger one. Tom. Got pregnant. And Roger and Eleanor... They were devastated. And then that night..." He trails off, picks up the whiskey again, then changes his mind, sets it down and pushes it away.

"That night..." I repeat, prompting him. Desperate for him to continue.

"That night. Billie, I— I told the police that your father pushed Will in. I thought he did. At first. It— It wasn't like that, though. Will fell. He was drunk. We both were. I'm sorry. I'm so sorry."

But the apology is drowned by a wave surging inside me. Of hope. Shining hope. And the insects pause in its wake.

"What?"

"Your father didn't push Will. He dived in to save him." He looks up and meets my eyes, wide with it, with disbelief. "He died trying to save him."

I stare at him. "You mean he didn't... He wasn't..." And

though I can't say the word, I feel the hope turn to relief, feel it flood my veins now, like warm whiskey, like courage.

"Tom loved your mother. And you. That much I knew. I always knew. I tried to tell her. I rang but…"

That phone message. That was why he called. And she deleted it. But it doesn't matter now. Because it's out. The last secret is out. That it wasn't because of her, or me. He didn't falter, didn't run, didn't hide. Didn't kill. He was a hero. He was my dad. And I need to know. Need to know him again. Everything. Starting with…

"His name," I say. "I've never known it. Tom. Thomas something."

He shakes his head. "Not Thomas," he says. "Tomlinson. Edward Tomlinson."

I let out a sound; a laugh, maybe. Tomlinson. Tom. That's why I couldn't find him. That's why I've never found him. I was looking for the wrong man.

"I have to go," Jonty says, rising, his chair scraping the tiles.

And I stand too, because I want him to go. Need to tell Danny. And Mum. Tell her she got it wrong. That he didn't leave. And that he loved her. He loved us.

"Call me," he says. "If you need anything."

"I will," I say. But I know it's a lie. Because what could I need now? I have everything.

I burst into the kitchen, my heart pounding, my words falling out of me now.

"It wasn't him," I blurt. "He didn't kill Will. He was saving him. Do you see? Saving him. He was a hero. My dad was a hero, Danny."

"Oh Billie." Danny takes me in his arms again, but I'm too full of news to let him hold me. "And his name. I got it wrong. It's not Tom."

"No?"

"No, that was just a nickname. It's Tomlinson. Edward Tomlinson."

And then it happens. Danny staggers backwards, as if I've punched him. Reeling in confusion, his eyes roll as he tries to find his feet.

"Danny?" I say. "What—?"

He holds on to the edge of a table. Bent over. "He had a brother," he says into the ground.

"Yes. James or something. But what's that—?"

"Jimmy," Danny murmurs.

I don't get it. And like an idiot, a child, I blurt out, "Who's Jimmy?"

Danny raises his head, looks at me, his face ashen, contorted.

And then my world drops away as, through a sob, I hear him say, "My dad."

TOM

TOM IS late. He is supposed to be at her house now. With his bag packed and his goodbyes said. Supposed to be throwing a stone at the window.

But he has to work. Has to stay late fixing an engine for Jimmy. Jimmy, who knows what he's planning. Knows he is leaving. And why.

Tom checks his watch. It is gone half ten already. He'll be done soon. There's still time, he thinks.

He hears them before he sees them. The staggering footsteps, the shouting, the jeering. Knows it is them. Can hear the plums in their mouths, the silver spoons, as they swill their beer.

They are drunk. Jonty's mouth gaping open, a trail of

saliva hanging, shining like a slug's trail, then snapping and dropping onto the wooden boards. The other one, her brother, is standing on the bottom rung of the railings like he's surveying his kingdom. The world that he has inherited. Not the meek.

Tom should leave them to it. Should walk away. Run, even. He doesn't have long. But what would she say if she knew? If something happened. So he does the right thing. And the wrong one. He tells him to get down.

Jonty turns. Sees who is standing there. "Eff off, Gyppo," he leers, lager swilling over his wrist as he tries to shoo him away.

Tom ignores him. "Seriously, Will," he says. "It's dangerous. You shouldn't be up on there."

"You know she's only using you," Jonty slurs on. "You're her bit of rough, that's all." He takes another swig.

Tom snaps. "She told me all about you," he says. "Couldn't stand you. Any of you. None of you have a clue what she wants. Who she is."

"And you do?" Jonty laughs.

"I do."

"Loser." Jonty takes a swing at him with the bottle, followed by fifteen stone of full back. But he's drunk. And Tom is fast. He ducks and Jonty pitches into the railings, hits the side of his head on the top bar and crumples into a heap.

"Shit," he groans.

"Pikey bastard."

Tom turns. Will has climbed over the railings and is

facing them now. Showing off. To him, to Jonty. An end-of-the-pier show with an audience of two.

"Will." Tom moves towards him. "You need to come back over."

"I don't need to do anything."

Tom holds out a hand.

Will punches it away.

"I don't want a fight," Tom insists. "I'm trying to help you."

"I don't need your help," Will sneers. "Look! No hands!" He lets go of the railings. Holds his arms out wide. Like an angel. Like Christ on the cross. Eyes staring blankly ahead.

"Will, stop it."

Tom lunges to grab him. But it is too late. Will falls backwards, plunging ten metres into the blackness below, hitting the water like a dead-weight, drink-heavy and helpless.

Tom turns to Jonty, but he is too far gone, no use to either of them. He tries to call out but the sound of the fair drowns him, the shrieks and music and clunking of machines. He can run. Or he can stay.

He has no choice. It is Het's brother. So he climbs over the railings, and jumps.

Will is panicking, his limbs thrashing in the blue-black ink. Tom grabs at him, but Will kicks out, sending the full force of a size eleven Timberland into his stomach.

Without thinking, Tom opens his mouth to scream. And as he does, the water rushes in, choking him. He tries to cough it out but a second wave hits him, sends him and Will crashing into the iron struts of the pier.

He sees Will's body go limp. Tries to swim towards him. But then he feels it, feels the suck of water around his legs. He grasps at a strut, but it is too quick for him, too clever.

The undertow has caught him. It is taking him down.

But he doesn't see a tunnel of light. Doesn't see long-dead things. Doesn't see angels. He sees Het. Waiting at the table. The clock ticking. Her belly swelling. Wondering where he has gone.

BILLIE

NAUSEA HITS me like a wave. Slamming into my diaphragm, knocking me against the wall and then out the door. I throw up in the gutter, twice, three times. Then retch, bringing up thin pale bile, and then nothing, my body heaving still, trying to get rid of this sickness. But I don't feel relief. Just empty. My *cousin*, I think. Not my true love, or destiny, or anything like that. We are the same because we come from the same. He is part of me. He is family.

I heave again, but there is nothing left.

"Billie."

I look up. And he is there. His face etched with shock.

"I'm so sorry," he tries. "I thought… Jones is my mum's name. I…"

But he can't speak. And I don't want to listen anyway. Can't listen.

The buzz of the neon signs on the arcades fills the space between us. Building to a crescendo in my head.

"Danny—"

But he stops me. "It doesn't have to change anything," he says.

I feel something hit my stomach again. Disbelief. Disgust. And I find my voice. "It changes everything, don't you see? Everything." I reach for the door.

"Billie, wait!"

But I'm gone.

I walk quickly, half running, but he doesn't follow me. All the while my head filled with thoughts, frantic creatures, beating their wings, battling to be heard. Why did it have to be him? Why not Eva? Or one of those kids from the arcade? Anyone. Anyone but him.

I'm a small-town cliché. I'm a joke. I hate it. Hate it here. I want to go home. I hate her for bringing us. And I hate myself for letting her.

I want to change it. To lose myself. Be someone else. Forget who I am. What I've done. I feel in my pocket to see what's left. A fiver. Enough for a bottle of Thunderbird. And I thank God that I am tall, tall enough to pass for eighteen; twenty-one, even. Though I guess I should thank my dad.

* * *

I sit on the pier, another stray from the fair. No one takes any notice here. He's in there, I think. My uncle. My real alive uncle. But the thought is bitter, tainted. And the wine is sweet and strong. It fills me with fire. I drink. I drink to drive the thoughts out. To forget. But I don't forget. Instead, I start to remember.

She knew.
Drink.
She knew who he was. That time at the piano.
Drink.
I saw it in her. A ghost. She had seen a ghost.
Drink.
She had seen my father.
Drink.
She lied. She's lied for years.
Drink.
If she'd told me his name, this never would have happened.

And I want an end. Even through the haze of the wine, this one thought is clear. I want an end to secrets. Because they don't stay buried. They come back. No matter how strong you are, how fast a swimmer, like an undertow, they twist around your ankles, and pull you down.

Het

HET IS in the kitchen. It is late. Her parents already in their beds, twins now, four feet and a thousand miles apart. She is watching the clock. Seeing the seconds, minutes, hours tick past. Seeing the plans she has made, the life she has imagined, dissolve before her, no more than candyfloss. A tiny crystal of sugar spun into something significant, beautiful. But shrinking on your tongue to nothing.

Maybe her mother is right, she thinks. That he is like his brother. Feckless. Flitting from one job to the next, one girl to the next.

Another hour passes, counted off in tiny increments, each tick tock *another nail of truth driving into her too-weak flesh.*

At eleven, she realizes it is over. He isn't coming.

She leaves the key on the table, heaves her rucksack onto her shoulders and walks out of the house, out of their lives. All that she needs is in this bag, and inside her.

At the gate she stops, turns and looks up at the window of her parents' room. The heavy velvet drapes drawn, no chink of light entering or escaping. When they wake, she will be gone, a memory. A bad dream, nothing more.

She turns and walks down the hill to the station. To the eleven-thirty sleeper to Paddington. To Martha's. To her new life.

BILLIE

FINN IS in the kitchen eating beans on toast.

He looks up. "Hey. Billie. I—"

"Where is she?" I interrupt. "Mum?" As if I could mean anyone else.

"Swimming," he says, chewing slowly.

And in that second I am sober. The blur of anger and alcohol snap into crisp, clear, panic. "But she can't," I say.

He swallows, tuts. "I don't know. Lessons, maybe. She said she wanted to learn. Remember?"

"Oh God."

I try to think. Where would I go? Where would I go if I'd just told my daughter her father was dead after all? That I'd been lying to her for years?

"The pier," I blurt out. "Finn, you need to get help. Get the police. Tell them to come to the pier."

"Why?" He's scared now. Scared of me. Can see me losing it again. But I don't have time to tell him.

"Just do it, Finn. Please, for me."

And then I run. I run until I can feel my heart bursting out of my chest, the pavement driving splints into my shin bones. I run until I get to the sea.

She's wearing a bikini. My bikini. People are staring. Queues of kids and parents at the candyfloss stand, at the coconut shy. All staring at her pale, goosepimpled flesh. Embarrassment pricks me again. Then shame. For what we've done. This is my fault too. I lied. Told her there was nothing between Danny and me.

I'm just a few metres from her now. Too scared to get closer in case she falls. Or jumps. "Mum," I say. "Mum, it's OK. Please come away. It's going to be all right."

But my words are lost in the crash of the sea. Spring tides have swelled its height and filled it with an anger I've not seen before.

But then something rises above them. A voice behind me. Close.

"Billie."

I turn to see Finn. But it's not the police he's brought with him. It's Danny.

"Finn—" I say in panic.

"I've called the police," Danny says. "They're coming."

Then Finn sees past me. Sees his mum in a red bikini. Standing at the railings in the freezing rain, the waves crashing across her bare legs. Sees her raise her arms, the fingers elegant, pointed, poised. Like she's a ballet dancer, a bird.

"Mum!" he cries.

But she doesn't hear him. She bends her knees, just a fraction, then pushes off, dives, graceful as a swan, into the clotted grey sky.

And it's like time has slowed, or stopped. Like those bits in films where the noise stretches into a gurgling yawn. But then her fingers pierce the inky black. And she is gone.

In an instant the film speeds up. Stuff happens really fast. Finn runs to the gap in the railings, and I reach to grab his coat to stop him, but he stumbles, trips on something, and falls, keeps on falling, following Mum's descent into the water.

And then I forget. Forget that I'm scared of the still, chlorine-clean swimming-pool, let alone a relentless sea. Forget that I can barely float on my back. I just know I have to help them. My family. So I take off my coat and boots. And I jump.

When I hit the water the cold takes my breath away. But it's nothing compared to the terror when the first wave hits me. Water floods my ears, my nose, my mouth. Its strength is overwhelming, carrying me metres in one easy roll. Under the pier, against one of the legs. I grab hold of it, of the rusted metal. Cling on, coughing, choking, as the sea tries to suck me back out again.

The cold seeps through my clothes, my hair. Like a creeping frost. Within seconds my fingers and toes are numb. Then my legs, pins and needles pricking them under my jeans.

I look around frantically. See a head bobbing on the surface. I have to get to it. Move, I tell myself. Move. I hear Danny's voice in my head instructing me. "Kick your legs, Billie. Move your arms, Billie. Billie. Billie. Billie."

"Billie."

I turn as I hear the voice again. It's not in my head. He's not in my head. He is in the water.

"Don't let go," Danny shouts. "I'm getting Finn."

And I watch as he pushes out into the water, across the waves, letting them pull him, then moving again, swiftly at an angle. I see him grab Finn. Lock an arm around his middle. Around his kicking and screaming eight-year-old body. Around my brother.

And then I see someone else. I see Will. And I see my dad, his arm around him, trying to pull him to the shore. See Will fighting him, kicking him off. I have to tell her. I have to let her know.

But it is too late. Because I can feel my frozen fingers loosen their grip on the pier. Feel the rip of the tide against the shelving sand. The pull of the water on my body. I can't fight it. I don't have the strength.

So I give in. I let it take me away. Wait for the water to flood my lungs. For everything to fade to black.

ELEANOR

ELEANOR ANSWERS *the door and, though he has rung to arrange the meeting, she still feels a wave of surprise run through her. It is the first time she has seen him since Roger's funeral. But she brushes it lightly away and paints a smile on her lips.*

"Jonathan," she says. "Come in."

At first she is angry. At the years of living a lie. At the truth that her own son was a bully. And a drunk. Like his father before him.

> *But he is gone. And she has cried her tears for him.*
> *But Het, Het is alive.*

* * *

She will find her, she thinks. She will drive to London and find her.

The minute the words fill her head, joy fills her heart. And she cannot stop herself. She packs a small case, enough for a night, two at most. She will find a hotel. Because it is too soon to stay. There is too much to be said. Too many explanations and apologies. And she will. She will apologize. For that night. And for the years before. The years of never holding her, never telling her that she loved her. Because she was hers.

Because she was his.

She will tell her that she has saved money. For her granddaughter. That she changed her will and opened an account. Put back the money that should have been Het's.

But first she has to tell Alex. Has to tell him everything. There are to be no more secrets. Because secrets aren't benign. They aren't just scratches in the table. Or a single kiss. They are dangerous things. Things that eat away at you, that, when you strive to hide them, beat louder, threatening to reveal themselves. Things that hurt.

Except this one, she thinks. For the hurt was done long ago. And now, this secret will heal.

BILLIE

AT SCHOOL once I wrote this story, some complicated thing with a witch and a dragon and a fairy-tale castle. Only I couldn't work out how to end it, so I just did that "And I woke up and it was all a dream" trick. And I guess I was waiting for that to happen. I thought I'd open my eyes and I'd be back on the sofa in Peckham under that faded duvet, watching Saturday-morning telly. That the post was just bills, that Mum and Finn would come back with bread and milk, that Cass would charge up the stairs with some raging hangover and a new lovebite and a "You won't believe what Ash did".

But it never happens like that. Life isn't like stories. At least, not the ones I read, or wrote.

I woke up on the pier, on the damp wood, coughing and puking seawater from my stomach and lungs. The coast-guard pulled me out. Then Mum and Finn and Danny, one by one. Our lips blue, our skin white.

The undertow didn't drag us under. But the past did. Got all of us in the end.

But we're not burying it this time. Not running away.

Luka came. Of course he came. With Nonna and Nonno and Martha in her clapped-out Toyota. They arrived just before they discharged Finn, packed him in the back, squashed between Nonna and me, and drove us all back to the house. Martha lasted a week before she missed the city. Better than Cass. She lasted a day. Came down on the train with a fake Prada suitcase and a biki-ni. Then said she couldn't stay 'cause she had school and everything. Everything.

But Luka stayed.

And Mum? Mum's getting treatment from this doctor up at the hospital. Private therapy. She's paying for it. With her own money. Martha found the bank book when she was cleaning. Fallen down the back of the book shelves. Fifty thousand in trust. Enough to pay the back rent, and the bills for years to come.

Money doesn't buy happiness, Martha said, but it buys you a big-enough boat to sail right up to it.

And Mum's doing OK. I told her the truth, about that

night. About Dad and Will. And she's talking about it all. And shouting. She rang up Jonty and shouted at him for ten minutes straight then hung up, and said, "That's closure."

I didn't lose my job. Debs said beggars can't be choosers and Lisa is signed off for six months with backache so she needs me three days a week. And I guess I don't need the money. But I need something to do.

Because I'm missing the rest of the school year. Finn, too. Mum said Luka can do some parenting for a change, instead of that bloody guitar.

But he's found a way round it. He set himself up doing music classes in that old gallery. Like *School of Rock,* or something. He plays with Danny too, sometimes. Says he's good. Says he can get him session work, if he wants.

But he doesn't. Not right now. Because that would mean going away. Going up to London. And neither of us wants that. Not yet.

We're not together. That would be too weird. But I came here to find out who I was. And I thought I needed to find my dad to do that. But instead I found Danny. He's part of my family now.

We could have ignored it. Could have run away. Together, or alone. But it would have pulled us back in the end. Like it did Mum. It's who we are. We can't change it. Or fight it.

We just have to find new ways to live. And to love.

ALEX

ALEXANDER SHAW *sits at the window, looking out over the forecourt of the garage. A girl, woman really, is filling her car with petrol.*

It's the car that jogs his memory. A Pallas. With fawn leather seats and a suspension that rose as you turned on the ignition. A strange sensation, he thought, as if you were being lifted in a space machine, a rocket.

He remembers the smell too. Of cigarettes and a plastic air-freshener, the liquid domed over the amber of a traffic light. Get set. And perfume. Her perfume.

She smelt of it that day. The last day he saw her.

"I have to go," she says. "I have to find her."

"I will come. Can I come?" he asks. He takes her hand in his own. Feels the fine-boned fingers, the hard gold of her wedding band, the chilled January.

She tightens her hand around his, feels the rough, calloused palm, the bone-swollen fingers. An artist's hands, she thinks. Hands that have coloured the wash of the sea with deft strokes of prussian and cobalt. Hands that have held her face as he kissed her. That have unzipped a navy dress, and touched the bare flesh beneath.

But that was then.

She brings her other hand to meet their grasp, closes it around them, then kneels beside him. Like Mary Magdalene, he thinks. Or a begging child, imploring him.

"No," she says. "No, you can't come. But I need to tell you something."

She stands now. Removes her hands from the tangle they have twisted themselves into.

"It's our secret," she insists.

He nods, then laughs. "I'll forget anyway."

It is the last time he sees her.

That evening a woman comes to see him, the one with the dark hair and the smell of pine needles. She tells him she is dead. Gone. There was an accident on the main road.

And for a second, then, he feels the sudden stab of pain, of loss. But by dinner-time he has forgotten. Forgotten her name, even.

* * *

But today he remembers. And he remembers their secret. I will write it down, he thinks. So I can tell her when she comes. Tell her who she is. That she is mine. My flesh and blood. My granddaughter.

What is her name? he asks, as he searches in the bedside drawer for a pencil.

Billie. That is it. Billie.

READ BETWEEN THE LINES

UNDERCOVER is the best
in young adult fiction from
Walker Books.

Scan this code to watch other
UNDERCOVER book trailers:

Get the mobile app
http://gettag.mobi

Turn the page to check out more
UNDERCOVER READS or visit
www.undercoverreads.com

Jude must get away.

She has to ace her exams and an audition at a prestigious drama school or she'll never escape her small town life and follow her dream of becoming an actor.

But then her best friend Stella returns, bringing excitement and danger to Jude's dull existence. For the first time, she can be who she wants to be. But as her life spirals out of control, Jude uncovers a dark secret. Will Stella save her – or destroy her?

Scan this code to read an extract from
wonderland

Get the free mobile app at http://gettag.mobi

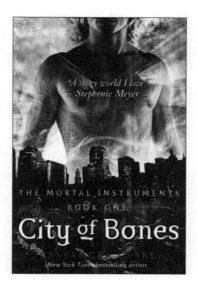

It's after dark in New York City, and Clary Fray is seeing things. The best-looking guy in the nightclub just stabbed a boy to death – but the victim has vanished into thin air. Her mother has disappeared, and a hideous monster is lurking in her apartment. With her life spiralling into darkness, Clary realizes that she has stumbled into an invisible war between ancient demonic forces and the secretive Shadowhunters – a war in which she has a fateful role to play...

"The Mortal Instruments series is a story world I love to live in. Beautiful." *Stephenie Meyer*

Lennie Walker – sisterless, lasagna maker,
Heathcliff-obsessed and hopelessly in love…

*What kind of girl wants to kiss every boy at a funeral, wants to
maul a guy in a tree after making out with her (dead) sister's
boyfriend the previous night? Speaking of which, what kind of
girl makes out with her sister's boyfriend, at all?*

"The book of the year … this book is perfection."
Carly Bennett (blogger)

"Heart-warming."
Independent

"Entirely compelling."
Guardian

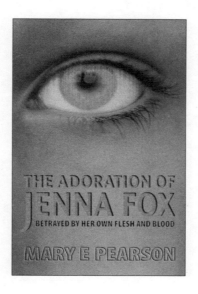

A girl wakes from a coma following a
devastating accident, her memory a blank.
One day she can't walk; the next she can.
One day her right eyelid droops; the next it doesn't.
Her parents call her recovery a miracle –
but at what cost has it come?
What are they hiding from her?
*Who **is** Jenna Fox?*

A GRIPPING PSYCHOLOGICAL THRILLER SET
IN A FUTURE THAT MAY BE CLOSER THAN WE THINK.

"This novel is truly unlike any other I have ever read
and is a breath of fresh air in the often predictable
world of teen literature." *ELLEgirl*